CW01066906

SEDUCTION

Cathryn Cooper

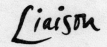

First published in 1997
by HEADLINE BOOK PUBLISHING

A HEADLINE LIAISON paperback

10 9 8 7 6 5 4 3 2 1

ISBN 0 7472 5627 6

Typeset at The Spartan Press Ltd
Lymington, Hampshire

Printed and bound in Great Britain by
Cox & Wyman Ltd, Reading, Berkshire

HEADLINE BOOK PUBLISHING
A division of Hodder Headline PLC
338 Euston Road
London NW1 3BH

SEDUCTION

Chapter 1

Virginia Vernon was intent on seduction, and to seduce was a matter of expediency. Her aim from a very early age had been to be rich and she had every intention of achieving this.

Unfortunately, or fortunately as the case may be, Virginia had not been born rich. With envious eyes she had seen those who lived in the big houses up on the hill and wore lace and smelt of lavender. Not for them a day out consisting of a tram ride to the suburbs or an annual treat being a charabanc outing to the seaside.

Most of those living on Nob Hill had one of the new motorcars that had shiny lamps and curving mudguards. Only the milkman, the baker and the grocer still used horses, and even the latter made more use of a boy on a bike with a large basket on the front.

It was those with the cars, the women with shingled hair and short skirts, that Virginia envied the most. They laughed a lot, danced the Charleston and the Black Bottom Rag and were referred to as bright young things.

The men they kept company with had slicked-back hair, wore striped blazers, boaters and Oxford bags that flapped like sails in the wind. They were also the ones who dined out, played tennis and holidayed in the South of France. They were the people who had been *born* with money and Virginia wished she'd been born with the same assets.

But she did have the assets bestowed on her by Mother

1

Nature. Virginia had dark hair, blue eyes and a face to be remembered. She also had a narrow waist, breasts that begged to be fondled and curving hips just waiting to be caressed.

Physical beauty obviously attracted lust but, coupled with a shrewd mind and an ebullient personality, it also attracted wealth.

By the age of eighteen she had gone out of her way to be seduced by a man of means. Servility to those of less intelligence and less beauty than hers had been hard to bear, so when the husband of her mistress presented her with a more attractive proposition than smoothing his wife's hair and ego, Virginia took advantage of it.

Instead of being a lady's maid wearing black wool stockings and plain serge dresses, she became a kept woman. Wool gave way to silk and serge to satin. All she had to give was her body, and that in a pursuit of which she was inordinately fond.

At the insistence of her lover, who in all honesty preferred her without any adornment, all her clothes were supplied by the best couturiers of London, Paris and Rome. His was the bank account that paid for the soft leather shoes, the silken underwear and expensive stockings. His were the hands that trembled as her cami buttons were undone, her knickers, garters and stockings rolled down her long legs and away from her body.

Alas, Virginia's good fortune and her lover's surfeit of youthful sexuality was short-lived. Perhaps his time had truly come, or perhaps his lust for her body had contributed to his demise, but by the time Virginia celebrated her twentieth birthday, her benefactor had died.

To the chagrin of his family and her obvious satisfaction, her beauty and her services had been amply rewarded. The kindly and licentious gentleman had left her a decent part of his wealth.

For the first time in her life, Virginia was a free spirit, her freedom that much greater because she had the wherewithal to please herself.

And pleasing herself was exactly what she intended doing. She had been fond of her dearly departed lover but, it had to be remembered, he *had* been older than her. Virginia was sensual as well as beautiful, and sometimes her sexual vigour had been more intense and more demanding than that of her lover. In the darkness of night, she had sometimes lain beside him as he slept and snored low and warm. She had run her hands down his back, followed the curve of his spine, the roundness of his buttocks, and the cluster of wiry hair that protected his sleeping manhood.

No matter that her passion, earlier satisfied, had surged with new longing. Deft as her fingers might be, seductive as her words of passion were against his ear, he never stirred – except to bend his knee and thus partially protect his sleeping softness.

Virginia now hungered for younger blood, a more virile disposition, and a body as firm as her own.

Being born into poverty and having tasted wealth had educated this engaging young woman. Although 1927 was the year of emancipation, Virginia was very much aware that if she was to maintain her lifestyle her new lover must also be a man of means.

But she had matured since that first liaison. This time she would make sure that her new benefactor was more suited to her in every respect. She was hungry for a man who could match her own desires, so this time she would sample what was available while her inheritance held out. That way, she reasoned, she would acquire the perfect partner; a man who would indulge her passions while at the same time providing her with a comfortable lifestyle.

With this in mind, she had considered where she could best find such a man. Mixing with London society was out of the question. There were too many wives and too many seasoned mistresses seeking a diminishing number of errant husbands. This was not because rich men were becoming more faithful, but because many men of substance had been cut down in the Great War.

It was after an evening at the opera that an option was presented to her.

Emerson, a rich Australian sheep farmer who had been showering her with presents and his sexual favours, was taking her home in a yellow Rolls-Royce complete with chauffeur. He had hired the whole ensemble for the duration of his visit.

Virginia had been enjoying the feel of his hand on her bare thigh and the shower of kisses he was scattering on her equally bare breasts. The traffic slowed suddenly and her attention was caught by a large poster outside Waterloo station.

Delicious things were being done to her nipples by Emerson's hot and very active tongue, so that at first she merely glanced at the poster.

What she saw immediately excited her. Some of the best artists of the decade had been employed to design such an eye-catching temptation to the jaded socialite. The image of a streamlined train running on abstract rails was incredibly potent.

Virginia was suddenly all attention. Though her body was being pleasured, part of her mind was still very alert and her eyes flicked wide as she took in the details.

Paris, Milan, Venice . . . and . . . what else did it say? Istanbul! Istanbul was the final destination of that streamlined train once it had steamed its way through the Balkans. The name of the train alone – Orient Express – made Virginia suddenly breathless.

As the traffic moved, a partner to the first poster further attracted her attention. This one showed very suave people being served by uniformed staff.

ORIENT EXPRESS, screamed the poster. In her mind she had already deduced that suave people were rich people.

Thus the idea of travelling to Istanbul was born. So was the idea that she didn't want to pay for it herself. She slid her gaze to the top of Emerson's dark-haired head. Substantial as her inheritance was, she was mindful of wasting it, and why waste it when men were so ready and willing to give her more? Given the right incentives of course.

'Emerson, darling,' she murmured, raising her wealthy Australian's head and kissing the tip of his nose before kissing his lips. 'You are the most exhausting lover I have ever had. Do you know that?' She sighed heavily and lay back to further emphasise her words. 'What a stallion you are, my darling.'

Like any man who has been told he's the greatest stud ever, Emerson's face fairly glowed with satisfaction.

'I can't say I've ever had any complaints,' he exclaimed proudly.

Virginia patted at her heaving bosom – not in line with Emerson's head, but just below her collarbone. 'My darling Emerson, you have been in London for only two weeks and in that time you have tired me out. You have used my body in every way possible and I am breathless, ecstatically wearied by your demands on me and the energy of my own desires.'

Emerson's blue eyes and tanned face looked bright enough to explode.

'My, Ginny old girl. You certainly do have a way with words. Beautiful they are. Do you really mean that?'

Virginia, pleased to see the man was vain enough to believe her every word, sighed. She looked at him through narrowed eyes as if she were too weary to open them any further.

'You have worn me out completely. Once you are gone back to Sydney or Brisbane, whatever, I will have to take a rest myself, and all because of you, you naughty boy!'

She flicked at his nose with her fingertip, her nail leaving a dent where it landed.

He grinned even wider than before, his face as bright as sunshine – Australian sunshine!

'You don't have to stay here, Ginny. Why not come with me? We could get married in Brisbane, have a bit of a honeymoon or some such before going to my station.'

'Your station?' A warning bell clanged in Virginia's mind. Emerson was rich. Good-looking too. But what exactly was this station?

'It's like a big farm,' he went on, his breath hot and wet between her breasts. 'I've got fifty thousand acres and just as many sheep. My land as far as the eye can see.'

'No neighbours?' asked Virginia, who already had some inkling of the answer.

'No. It's my place. Me and the shearers and a few black boys. I can honestly say you'd be the only woman for two hundred miles in any direction.'

A pang of fear took a sudden hold on Virginia's heart. Emerson was wealthy. There was no doubt of that. And beneath his evening dress there was a real man made of firm flesh, and taut muscles. Virginia's body quaked at the thought of it, of his flesh against hers, of his penis in her.

Emerson was everything she could want, but could she bear to live in some hot, dry place with only sheep and rough men for company? The answer was no. But was there another alternative?

'Do you have to go back?' she asked him. 'Couldn't you sell up and stay here?'

His response was instant. He shook his head vehemently. 'No, old girl. Couldn't do that. How would I make a living here in the old country? And, besides, who'd look after my sheep? Couldn't you think again about coming back with me?'

Virginia shook her head. 'I couldn't possibly go, Emerson darling. I get prickly heat in a British summer. Imagine what I'd look like in an Australian one? I'd be covered with

6

red blisters all over and you wouldn't love me any more, now would you?'

She stroked his hair as she waited for his response. A sudden feeling of sadness came upon her. 'I'll miss him,' she thought to herself, and that surprised her. It was something she had not expected to feel.

There was a small moment when his face froze. Virginia imagined that a vision of a pimpled woman, all naked and red, had shot through his mind before his smile returned.

'But I did ask you . . . I did ask you, Ginny.'

Virginia did not allow the relief to show on her face. She only smiled and said, 'Oh, yes, Emerson darling. You did ask me, and I love you for it. But I have had two weeks of your body, two weeks I will never forget for the rest of my life.'

Emerson's face was a picture. Adoration glowed in his eyes as though he were some star-struck adolescent and not a man nearing thirty.

'Wow, Ginny,' he exclaimed. 'You know what? You're the greatest too. Bloody marvellous you are. Best bint it's ever been my privilege to fuck!'

Virginia sighed again. She was pleased with herself and even more pleased that this man, like a lot of men she had known, measured his worth on a phallic scale rather than an intellectual one. It was regrettable that she had not been able to persuade him to stay and keep her in style and in sex. On the other hand she had avoided accompanying him to the back of beyond. There was no alternative now but to take the Orient Express in an effort to find herself a new lover. But first Emerson must offer her the finance. He was in her sights. Now for the final arrow.

'I shall most definitely need a holiday once you are gone – or I would if I could afford it.'

The grin on Emerson's face was slow in fading, but eventually it did.

'You short of readies, Ginny girl?'

'Short! I should say I'm short. I shall need a treatment of tonic and a thorough going over by my physician. After the way you have used my furry little cleft, he will need to examine me thoroughly. After all, I have to make sure all will be in order for when you return from the colonies. It will be a while before I'm my old self again and treatment will cost a fortune. I shall tell the doctor that it was all your fault. "I've been ravished by some sheep-farming bush-man," I shall tell him, "some handsome colonial boy with broad shoulders and a very big cock." After commiserating with me, he will take my money and that will be that.'

To add extra effect, Virginia covered her eyes with her arms and groaned – just like they did in the movies – all drama, all connivance. From beneath her arm, her eyes viewed him, waiting for his reaction.

Emerson fell for it completely. By the following Monday, two thousand pounds had been deposited in her bank account and Virginia was waving Emerson goodbye as he boarded the Southern Cross at Southampton.

Paper streamers tied the big white liner to the land. Throngs of people on the quay waved to those crowded along the bright, white rails of the ship and a band of Royal Marines played Auld Lang Syne.

'I'll see you again,' Emerson called out to her as he waved from the crowded deck.

Virginia smiled and blew him a kiss. To her surprise, her vision was blurred by what seemed to be tears.

'Don't be silly,' she muttered to herself as she dabbed at her eyes. 'Haven't you got what you wanted?'

And so she had. Sitting in her account at Coutts was the money to avail herself of the luxury of staying at the George V in Paris prior to boarding the Orient Express.

'You're a honey,' she had told Emerson before he had boarded the ship. 'You're a tart,' she had told herself, 'but', she added as she fingered her bank book, 'you're a well-off tart.'

'So why do I feel sad?' she asked herself. Her eyes misted over again as the big ship eased away from the dock to face the open sea and a six-week voyage to the other side of the world.

Chapter 2

While dining in the gold and white opulence of a hotel that had become synonymous with the look and sound of money, Virginia appraised those eating. Who did she care to seduce and who was worthwhile seducing?

There they all were, the stylish and beautiful guests of the George V. Dressed in silk and satin, wearing sharply cut evening suits with gold teeth flashing and smoke from Turkish cigarettes encircling their heads like transparent veils, they simply reeked of money.

They ate oysters, caviar, drank brandy and champagne. Gilt-edged voices spoke of shares, gold, bauxite and diamonds as they waited to join the most beautiful, the most exotic and, if rumours were to be believed, the most erotic train in the world. The Orient Express would whisk them through Milan, Venice, Trieste, Belgrade, Sofia and all the way to Istanbul, the city which had once been called Constantinople and straddled two continents.

Cleavages peered provocatively above plunging neck-lines. Nipples shone like pink medals through satin, silk and muslin. Eyes met eyes, spoke volumes, and moved on. Sensuality buzzed like a low voltage current through air rich with smoke and well-tutored voices.

Some of those who laughed and lounged were titled, their wealth passed down through the centuries. Others were the nouveau riche, acolytes and anointed of the second decade of the twentieth century.

Virginia eyed the gathering through narrowed eyes, her

fingers caressing the long rope of pearls that hung down over her breasts and reached beyond her navel. Her gaze flitted over them all and her expression never changed. It didn't matter that some met her eyes. It didn't even matter that she found one or two definitely worthy of seduction. Her eyes gave no hint of such a thing. Neither did she smile.

Her fine fingers tapped on the ebony holder through which she smoked her Passing Cloud. Her preference for English tobacco set her apart from the others. So did the thoughts that went through her mind as she assessed those gathered behind a pall of bluish smoke.

Just occasionally her glance lingered and so did her mind. 'I would imagine you have a good body beneath that suit,' she thought to herself.

The man she was eyeing saw her watching him. His eyes sparkled.

The Honourable Davis Sedglingham felt a rush of blood through his whole body. He had a sudden urge to flex his muscles, to breathe heavily regardless of who might hear him. There was a familiar tightening in his stomach, a stirring in his groin.

'Sweet girl,' he thought to himself. 'I wonder if she's travelling all the way to Istanbul? I wonder what chance I have of seducing her as we journey to the sun and the intoxicating splendour of the Orient? My, but just the thought of this journey inspires me.'

On this occasion, Virginia let her blue eyes linger. She smiled at him, caught his interest, then looked away.

'Don't make your mind up just yet, darling,' she told herself. 'Hold yourself aloof. See what transpires. Remember, there will be other men on that train, other bodies to imagine naked, hard and warm to lie beside on cotton, silk or satin sheets.' Satin for preference, she decided. Satin had such a sensual quality, almost as though it had fingers and caressed the body which lies on it. Oh yes, satin sheets for preference.

The man she had been studying shrugged his shoulders and went back to the newspaper he had been reading.

'A pretty girl, Davis,' he thought to himself, 'but just another in a world of pretty girls.'

Of course, if she was an heiress he might very well renew his acquaintance with her. But first he would make enquiries.

A waiter brought fresh coffee. Virginia saw his hand tremble as he poured and knew he was looking at her from beneath dark lashes.

'What is your name?' she asked, the word pouring from her tongue like warm toffee.

She saw the man stiffen before he answered.

'Raymonde, mademoiselle.'

'Tell me, Raymonde, are you open to bribery?'

He stared. Blinked. 'Mademoiselle?'

'You heard me, Raymonde. Are you open to bribery?'

'Mademoiselle . . .! That . . . that depends on . . .'

'Nothing illegal, Raymonde. Nothing very naughty.'

She laughed, a low, throaty sound that a man would love to hear on the pillow beside him.

Raymonde trembled visibly.

'Naughty, mademoiselle?'

Her voice became very soft. Very low.

'Pour my coffee and, as you pour, tell me who that man is over there.'

She pointed the tip of her cigarette in the direction of Davis Sedglingham.

Raymonde's eyes followed the direction in which she was pointing.

'Him,' Virginia said softly. 'The man hiding behind the newspaper.'

'Ah, yes, mademoiselle. I believe that is Mister Sedglingham. He is an "honourable".'

'Is he indeed? And is he going to Istanbul?'

'Yes, mademoiselle. Everyone here is going to Istanbul.'

The waiter still held the saucer of her coffee cup. Virginia

13

let her fingers wander across the table to deftly brush against his. She heard him gasp.

'Raymonde. Bring me chocolates next; the small Belgian ones filled with praline. And when you bring them, I will have another question to ask you.'

'Yes . . . Yes. Certainly mademoiselle.'

Raymonde's trousers were very tight across his buttocks. Virginia enjoyed watching him as he walked away from her. A swing door opened and he was gone. Beyond was some secret serving area where everything that the likes of her and her kind could want was stored and shared out in preordained proportions.

Virginia, whose eyes were violet blue and whose hair was black as a raven, set her gaze on another gentleman. Her glossy red lips smiled through the rising smoke. This man was different to the other, but no less handsome, no less a man for all that.

His hair was slick with shine and oil. Even at this distance she could imagine him smelling of lavender. He had brown eyes and an Italian look about him. Although his clothes spoke money, the look in his eyes and the way he puffed on an extra large cigar told her his country, his origin and his profession. American, she decided.

She smiled at him still as she thought it.

He winked before puffing on his cigar.

The brash blonde who sat beside him, wearing bright red satin which exactly matched her lipstick, glared. Virginia experienced a perverse enjoyment in watching the girl's fingers tightening around a butter knife.

Virginia kept her own counsel. In her mind she was imagining this man with brown eyes without his snappy suit and silk shirt. 'Brown skin,' she thought, 'and he's hairy. I just know that he's hairy. And imagine how broad his shoulders are and how hard his muscles.' His body would reflect his life. Where other men might have moles or freckles, he would have scars.

Not once did she deign to return the savage glare of the brassy blonde. Instead, she returned the American's wink, then tossed her head as she had before and let her gaze wander.

Raymonde chose that moment to return.

'Your chocolates, mademoiselle.'

Virginia let her eyes wander to Raymonde's face. She saw his lips tremble, his tongue lick the dryness.

'Thank you, Raymonde. Now. Tell me who that man is? The one with the cheap little blonde on his arm.'

'He is an American, mademoiselle. From New York. His name is Al Hutchinson. I am not sure of the woman's name. I think it is Honey. That what I have heard him call her, though in the register she is Mrs Hutchinson.'

'For sure?'

She shot him an enquiring look. Raymonde took her meaning.

'Only in writing,' he confirmed. 'This hotel does not require any proof of a man being wedded to the woman he is with. It would cause too many embarrassments, mademoiselle.'

She saw him blush and covered her smile with her hand.

'You have been of great service, Raymonde. But there are other questions I wish to ask. Will you come back to me in a few minutes?'

'Of course, mademoiselle. Anything to oblige.'

There was fresh meaning in the fiery look he gave her. She guessed his body was as fiery as his eyes.

'*Merci beaucoup*, Raymonde.'

'*Enchanté*, mademoiselle.'

Virginia went back to watching and surmising. One man pretended he had not been looking in her direction, yet she knew he had.

It had been just the briefest of glances, the furtive look of someone assessing, surmising, someone loath to betray his interest.

Married, she decided, but not uninterested. Now what sort of man was he?

Subdued elegance suggested a man who dealt in money on a daily basis; a banker, perhaps Swiss. A man used to handling vast amounts of other people's wealth and other people's secrets, all stowed away in neat little iron boxes with small keys and secret combinations.

As she turned her head away from him, she smiled in the same secretive way that he had looked at her.

She wanted to know this man's name too, but Raymonde had been waylaid by a woman whose figure resembled a well-risen cottage loaf. 'How inconvenient,' she thought with a frown.

'*Garçon*.' She said the word alluringly. She could just as easily have been addressing a lover. Raymonde was immediately at her side, his eyes shining with the need to serve her in whatever way she wanted. The other woman exclaimed her irritation and threw a none-too-friendly look in Virginia's direction.

'Mademoiselle?'

'Crème de menthe with fresh mint and crushed ice.' Her look was seductive, her voice provocative.

Raymonde made a move to leave.

'Come closer,' she whispered, and crooked her finger.

'Now tell me the name of the banker.'

Raymonde opened his mouth to speak. His eyes followed the movement of her red-nailed fingers as they curled over his arm. It was as if they were binding him to her. His gaze went back to her face. Coal-black eyelashes seemed to stretch to her eyebrows as she gazed up at him.

Unknown to him, she saw his waistcoat move, knew his stomach muscles were knotting as his penis sucked the blood from his body and became hard. He was, she realised, her immediate slave.

'Those too,' she said suddenly, and nodded to where two

16

men, obviously twins, had just entered the dining room. 'I want to know about them too.'

'They are new arrivals, but I will find out what I can. Shall I bring you the information later?' He blushed suddenly. 'Perhaps I could come to your room.'

'Perhaps you could, and not just with information about those men. You have served me well, Raymonde. Now, perhaps, it is time for me to serve you. *N'est-ce-pas?*'

Raymonde seemed almost to choke on his Adam's apple before he spoke. But, true professional that he was, he remained polite, and bowed out of Virginia's presence, his heart pounding in his chest and his penis thudding against his trouser buttons.

Virginia was hardly aware of him leaving. Her eyes were now assessing and snaring the two young men who took seats at a table to her right.

They returned her gaze, though their mouths did not smile, their flesh did not burn. Yet there was promise in their eyes and because of this she knew it would also be in their bodies.

Twins. What a picture they presented. Imagine setting one against the other. Imagine having them either side of her in the same bed on the same satin sheets. One brown body one side, one the other. What a delicious thought – and not necessarily a mere fantasy.

Nothing was impossible as far as Virginia was concerned. A long train journey lay ahead of her. Venice and Istanbul beckoned as the Orient Express pounded the rails from Europe to Asia. She would have time to explore these people more intimately than the countries she would travel through.

Chapter 3

Raymonde paused outside Virginia's door and wiped his palms over his hips before he knocked. His heart was pounding in his chest. Visions of what might transpire on the other side of that closed door – within her room – rattled through his brain in quick succession. The effect of those visions were evident and, although he might have wiped the sweat from his palms, he could not wipe away the seeds of sexual apprehension that stirred in his loins.

He heard her say enter, but before he laid his hand on the door knob, he wiped his palm again.

'Damn it man,' he muttered. 'Pull yourself together!'

After taking a deep breath, he patted at the stiffness in his trousers before his hand again reached for the knob. In one quick movement the door was open and what he saw made him stop in his tracks.

In the middle of the room was a chaise longue; a dramatic affair of warm cherrywood and blue brocade. But it was not the piece of furniture that had his attention, but the sweep of Virginia Vernon's naked hip, a sweeping curve of flesh infused with a warm, creamy glow.

One look was not enough. He stopped, stared, looked at the whole of her, and also took in the details of those parts of a woman a man cannot resist.

Black, silky and begging to be touched, nuzzled and kissed, her pubic hair nestled between her thighs. Raymonde was suddenly very hot, yet his body shivered.

His gaze travelled up over her flat belly to her breasts that were no more than an honest man's handful.

The colour of her nipples matched her lipstick which to him seemed strange, until he realised they had been rouged with the same hue.

She smiled knowingly, and suddenly Raymonde felt small, shy – like a little boy on his first day at school who must be instructed, told exactly what to do before he can truly take part.

'Raymonde, my darling man. Please. Close the door. Come in.'

Her voice was as languorous as the sweeping gesture of her arm which was long, curved like a swan's neck, and just as white.

Once the door had slammed shut behind him, Raymonde's arms fell uselessly to his side and his jaw fell open.

'Gee whizz,' he exclaimed, his voice trembling.

Now it was Virginia's turn to look surprised.

'Why, Raymonde! Do I detect that you are not quite as French as you pretend to be?'

The waiter swallowed as he shook his head. He took a deep breath. 'It really is Raymonde, though everyone back home calls me Ray. My mother was from Quebec. My father was from New Jersey.'

Virginia threw back her head and laughed.

Raymonde's eyes went to the long whiteness of her throat. In that instant he had an insatiable urge to kiss its firmness, to lick along her collarbone as his fingers explored her breasts. But those violet eyes were back upon him before he could move.

'Raymonde. You're an imposter! But never mind. How apt that is in a hotel full of imposters; of people pretending to be something they are not.'

She pursed her pretty red lips and, looking suddenly thoughtful, rested the tip of her finger against them. Suddenly she seemed to come to a decision. Resting one

20

arm on a heap of silk cushions, she raised herself up and swung her legs to the floor.

'Come here.' Her voice seemed to purr as she patted the space beside her.

Raymonde did exactly as was expected of him, his legs seeming to buckle as he lowered himself down. He sat next to her and was aroused by the thought she had just lain there. The warmth of her flesh had been left behind and was oozing through his trousers. She came closer.

'You have a very pretty complexion, Raymonde. Your flesh has been touched by plenty of fresh air. Your skin has a hint of sunburn about it, but your cheeks are slightly pink – like ripe plums. I like that. I like that very much.'

Raymonde's jaw trembled as her fingers swept down over his cheek, her thumbnail tracing the corner of his mouth.

'I like your cheeks too,' he managed to say, his voice shaking with emotion. 'But I like your nipples much more.' He dared to drop his gaze.

Virginia smiled and her eyes sparkled. Seduction was an elixir to her. Seeing a man fall under her spell was what she lived for, what she strived for. This man was too easy. All the same, he was very worthy.

'Tell me,' she said throatily, her breath hot against his ear, 'did you find out who those twins were?' She felt the hair on his neck bristle as her fingers caressed his flesh.

Raymonde gulped before he answered.

'Aristo and Ariel Kostopoles. They are Greek. Apparently they own a whole bunch of ships. Freighters mostly.'

Virginia raised her eyebrows. 'No luxury liners? Oh, how sad. But still, perhaps there might be more of a future in freight than in liners. Who knows how long people can go on indulging their whims in an ever-changing world?'

Raymonde shivered. His fingernails were digging into his palms. He wanted to touch her, yet was afraid to do so. His head was pounding. His flesh was burning.

'Tell me,' he heard her say. 'Do you think I should seduce them?'

She had a wicked smile on her face as she said it. Raymonde was sure he was being baited, played with, yet there was nothing he could do about it.

'One at a time, or both at once?' he managed to say, his voice showing a self-assurance he did not feel.

Virginia laughed. 'As yet, my dear Raymonde, I haven't made my mind up. What do you think?'

Raymonde licked at his very dry lips. 'I find that difficult to answer. I think you will do exactly as you please.'

Virginia nodded slowly.

Raymonde caught his breath. Because her head was nodding like that and her red lips were parted, he had an urge to grab hold of her hair and direct her mouth down into his lap. His member was throbbing so much that the buttons of his flies were digging into his flesh.

'You have been of great service to me, Raymonde. Do you know that?'

Her hand stroked his hair. He wanted to groan with pleasure and tell her to do much more to him, but he could not. After all, he was only a servant, a waiter working in this hotel. And she was . . .

He didn't know what she was. He only knew that he wanted her like crazy.

From somewhee deep inside he brought forth the courage to tell her what he had come for.

'I do know that, mademoiselle, and I am very glad that you are satisfied with what I did for you. Now I have come for the payoff.'

Virginia frowned. 'Payoff?'

He nodded in a swift jerky way that almost hid the turmoil he was feeling inside. It was very hard to keep his eyes off her body. His palms remained sweaty.

'Payoff is a term hoods use back in the States. It means a kickback, a token in exchange for what has been received.'

For a moment he wished the ground would swallow him whole. Virginia was staring at him in disbelief. Then slowly, very, very slowly, a smile returned to her plush, red lips.

'So, my darling Raymonde. You are saying that because I have received something from you – i.e. information – now it is your turn to receive from me. Is that what you are saying?'

Raymond nodded vigorously. 'Yes. That is exactly what I am saying.'

'I am not a person unable or unwilling to honour my debts, Raymonde. I will give you a little something in return for what you gave me.'

As her lips met his, her hand wandered across Raymonde's thigh and, at last, Raymonde groaned with pleasure. His penis leapt beneath her touch.

Infused with the sensuality of it all, he played with her breasts, his fingers pulling and tweaking on her nipples so that her body writhed against him and her moans were lost on his tongue. The scent of her inspired him as her hair brushed over his face. He wanted to eat her, be part of her, melt into her.

She eased her hips onto his lap and he caressed the firm flesh of her beautiful bottom. Her lips left his and she lay full stretch, her bottom resting in his lap, her pubic hair immediately before his gaze. He ran his fingers through it, luxuriating in its silky crispness. Its perfume rose up to him and its honey ran over his fingers as he prised between her folded lips.

'You have such a delicate touch, Raymonde,' Virginia moaned. 'You thrill me with it. You make me feel I am melting.'

So saying, she eased her legs apart so he could view her most inner jewels, his fingers folding back her outer lips. His thumb tapped at her clitoris. He felt it harden as though it truly were a small penis, a tiny reflection of the hardness that throbbed in his groin. In much the same way, his

23

fingers became his penis. He smeared the moistness of her body over the satin pink folds of flesh. Once he was sure that she was wet and ready for him, he slid his fingers into her. She gave a little cry – just as she would have done if it had been his member. And he lunged his fingers more deeply into her.

'This is much more than I hoped for,' he thought to himself as his breathing became more rapid. Within the close confines of his trousers, his penis rose hard and demanding.

'Do you like my pussy?' she asked him breathlessly.

'Oh, yes,' he murmured, the words sticking in his throat. 'It is very pretty.'

Virginia laughed. 'A pretty pussy. How sweet. How very original!' Then her voice again subsided into moans of delight and her hips danced to the rhythm of his fingers.

He did not know for sure whether she was making fun of him, but he took advantage of the sudden raising of her hips by pushing his other hand beneath her bottom.

Now he could feel the tight crease between her buttocks, the plumpness of her cheeks against his hand. Her sex was his entirely and he was enjoying feeling its wetness and its warmth.

Virginia's hands began to circle her breasts as he did these luscious things to her. She was mewing with delight, her eyes closed, her hips undulating in his lap as his hands continued to play with her.

As he watched and listened, his own ardour becoming too much to bear, a sudden thought occurred to him. He was giving to her. She was not giving him anything. That was not the deal, he told himself, and vowed to do something about it.

And yet he did not want to disturb her concentration. What was more, he did not want to stop this from happening, did not want her to tell him to stop.

With each roll of her bottom against his hand, he undid

the buttons of his trousers and eventually pulled his penis from its warm lair.

Virginia continued to raise her hips up and down to meet the hand that played with her sex and the one that played with her behind.

Once more she rose and, as she came down, Raymonde's penis was there to meet her, its glistening head forcing aside the cheeks of her behind.

She gasped, but with the hand that pleasured her sex Raymonde held her steady.

Her eyes rolled back in her head and she groaned loudly, almost protestingly, as his penis entered her smallest orifice. Yet she did not protest. In fact, her body jerked more vigorously against him, her juices flowed more copiously, which in turn made his invasion of her behind a lot easier.

His hands gripped more tightly at her breasts as his length inched aside the tightness of her flesh. Once he was embedded as far as he could go, his own hips began to jerk up and down against her.

They were like some odd automaton, some creation of a mad toymaker, wound up with an invisible key that made their bodies thrust and slap together.

Virginia cried out at times. Some cries were high and piercing, some mere mews of delight. At times she threw her arms above her head, her hands clasping and unclasping at the air – as if that would help her endure this or enjoy it more.

Intermittently, her hands returned to grip at her breasts. And sometimes her fingers entwined with Raymonde's, whose free hand now had leave to explore her creamy flesh while his other hand applied pressure to her clitoris.

Now they were in unison, their bodies taken on a tide of passion that rose and broke, rose and broke again and again.

Raymonde could now use his hand to push her down to meet his demanding penis. Her juice ran over his fingers, down through her sexual lips to lick at the base of his stem.

Eddies of electricity ran up from his groin as his semen rose hot and anxious up through his member. So intense were his sensations that he wanted to close his eyes, to drown in them, to enjoy this scenario by touch alone. But he could not do that. He found it impossible to tear his eyes from her body. It was like reading music. He had to study the melody of her body in order to enjoy the tune that came from his own.

There was no protest from the woman he was using to achieve his orgasm. She made no effort to escape that which invaded her behind or that which invaded her vagina. She rode with it all and when her climax came it made her body quiver like a creature impaled, shudders of delight running like iced water over her flesh.

With one last thrust of his hips, Raymonde released his fluid and felt it gushing like a fountain into her body.

For a while she lay there, soft, pliant, her limbs completely relaxed, her eyes closed as her breathing slowly returned to normal.

Even now, Raymonde could not stop looking at her, draped like some exhausted animal across his lap.

'Yes,' he thought to himself. 'Like some exhausted animal. Some wild creature hunted to exhaustion. That's what she looks like. And yet, I know that I am not the hunter and she is not the hunted. She is both, and I – and many men like me – are her prey.'

'So why are you in Paris, Raymonde – Ray? Are you studying here?'

He laughed. 'Nothing so positive. I'm just an adventurer, a guy from the sticks looking for a little excitement. Perhaps even a little decadence.'

Virginia's eyes flashed open and looked at him over the rise of her naked breasts.

'In Paris? My darling man, how can you expect to find decadence in Paris? It is so civilised, so very French. A husband has his mistress, a wife has her lovers. What is

26

decadent about that? In Paris, as in a large part of France, it is the norm not the exception. Therefore it is no longer decadent but routine.'

He shook his head at her logic. 'My, but your philosophy is too much for me. Though I do take your point. So where do I go to find this decadence?'

Virginia swung her legs to the floor and cuddled against him. She kissed his ear.

'Come with me, my darling man. Travel with me to the Orient with a group of people who I know to be the last word in decadence.'

He turned his head so that their chins rubbed together. He was aware that his was already showing the first signs of dark stubble – not that it seemed to worry Virginia. Her breath was tantalising against his hair, her tongue wet and enticing as it darted around his ear lobe.

'You mean the other passengers going on the Orient Express?'

'Ye . . .sss,' she said slowly on a long hiss of breath. 'Take it from me, they are all decadent characters with diverse but debauched natures. Trust me.'

Raymonde thought of the six by eight room he was sharing with the commis chef who had smelly feet and snored. He also thought of the few francs he had left and the old dowagers he would have to service to the hilt before he got any more. He thought of the softness of their flesh, the dryness of their copulating.

'And what will this cost me?' he asked.

Smiling in a secretive, sexy way, Virginia shook her head. Her lips brushed his. She looked into his eyes and wondered if he could see the glint of an idea in hers. She also wondered how he would react to her suggestion.

'Nothing,' she whispered. Her tongue darted at his ear. 'Nothing, as long as you play along with my game.'

Chapter 4

Virginia Vernon was pleased with herself. Not only was she now boarding the Orient Express for its long, cross-continental journey to Istanbul, but she had acquired a companion to take with her.

'Come along, Dorothy. Leave that luggage with the porter. There's no need to prove to him just how strong you are.'

The woman addressed as Dorothy looked suddenly embarrassed about attempting to heave two heavy valises onto the porter's trolley. The porters, liveried in their bright blue uniforms, tailed jackets a leftover from the last century, leapt into immediate action.

With clumsy attention to her black velvet hat and an ungainly stride, the woman in the unfashionably long dress and fur-trimmed coat followed Virginia up the steps and onto the most famous express train in history.

The men of means Virginia had studied back at the hotel watched the lithe form in the dark green suit. The skirt she wore was fashionably short and pleated. Her close-fitting hat and huge wrap of a coat was edged with fur and opened in an inverted "vee" to reveal her skirt. An ornate clasp of silk edged with silver held it together beneath her breasts.

Virginia moved with the sexual grace of someone aware of her own magnetism. The men responded accordingly, their parted lips a sign of how, in their minds, they were touching her and tasting her. What did they care that she had now acquired some gawky woman to protect her honour on the long journey? Their desire was too hot to worry about such a minor detail.

'Well will you look at that, Al, baby,' growled the so called Mrs Hutchinson to her so called husband. 'That broad you were eyeing's got another woman with her now. Big she is too. That's to protect her from wolves like you!'

Al Hutchinson tore his eyes away from Virginia Vernon who he was lusting after like mad, his prick hot and hard against his belly. He glared at Petula and his mouth widened into an ugly grin.

'Is that so?'

Petula squealed as his iron-hard fingers gripped her arm. Her eyes, heavy with make-up, opened wide.

'Less of yer sass, honey,' he growled. 'Or you'll be going home courtesy of International Mailing – in pieces. And get this straight, no old broad stands between me and what I want. She can damn well watch if she likes. And so can you! Al Hutchinson always gets what he wants. You should know that well enough, baby!'

Petula's bright red lips pouted like a child on the verge of tears. At the same time, she whined like a jammed mincer.

'Shut that noise up and get aboard!' Al snapped, and Petula, mink coat flying open to reveal a pink satin dress that looked more suited for evening wear than travelling, obeyed without further protest. Even when his hand punched into her backside to make her get up the step that much quicker she did not protest. She merely followed the car attendant and, once in their cabin, huddled herself in a corner seat and stared red-eyed over the top of her coat collar. With childish petulance she sniffed and sniffed again. Then, just as a sob was about to break, she shoved her hand up to her chin and began to suck her thumb.

Al grabbed hold of her. 'Knock it off. I don't want no grizzling from some snivelling broad. I'm on vacation, baby, and I want to enjoy it. Anyone that spoils my enjoyment is liable to feel the back of my hand. Do you get me?'

Petula sniffed and managed to nod.

Al smiled. 'That's better.'

As the train began to move, he let go of her chin and began to pull down the blinds in their private compartment.

'Now, baby. Let's say we start this vacation as we mean to go on.' Once the light from the windows was completely obliterated, the broad-shouldered American turned round and smiled in the same way a dog sneers before it takes a bite of a marrowbone. 'Take your coat off and bend over.'

The fear in Petula's eyes became less intense. She managed a weak smile before doing as ordered.

He took her coat from her and flung it somewhere behind him.

Hands on seat, feet on floor, Petula fixed her eyes on the pale grey and blue of the seat's velvet covering.

Without a kiss or the slightest hint of foreplay, she felt Al's rough hands pulling her skirt up over her behind until it lay in a rumpled heap around her waist.

Two real bone buttons made a popping sound and bounced on the floor as Petula's pale pink camiknickers were ripped from her equally pink bottom.

His fingers gripped and pinched the white expanse of flesh between bottom and stocking tops until her whimpers were a mixture of sobs and moans.

'That's it, honey,' he growled. 'Let me hear you cry for me. Let me hear you suffer for me.'

His grip lessened while he fiddled with his own buttons and pulled on his penis.

'Come here, honey,' he grunted. 'Get this into you!'

She braced herself as his thick fingers gripped her haunches and pulled her back onto his even thicker member.

She threw back her head and cried out as, with one almighty heave, he embedded himself in her unprepared body.

'That's it, honey. It's all yours!' he cried, his head back, his eyes closed and his face creased with cruel delight. And as he pushed and pummelled against her naked flesh, Petula squeezed her eyes tightly shut and pretended it was someone she loved.

In their cabin, Aristo and Ariel Kostopoles settled down quickly either side of a table, heads almost meeting. Without saying a word, Aristo flung a ten franc note at the attendant. Ariel slammed a pack of cards down on the table.

'Aces high?' Ariel asked.

Aristo nodded. Both brothers kept their gaze firmly fixed on the deck of cards.

Ariel shuffled first. Aristo followed. The cards sat between them.

'I will go first,' Ariel announced.

'You always do,' remarked his brother.

'I was born first,' Ariel countered.

'You always say that.'

Ariel lifted the cards and slipped one into his other hand. He held it tightly against his chest until his brother had done the same. Only when this was done did the two brothers meet eye to eye.

Still holding his brother's gaze, Ariel flicked his card onto the table.

'Ten of diamonds.'

Aristo looked down at his card and then up into his brother's face. He showed no sign of what he was thinking until, in the same casual style of his brother, he let his card flick to the table.

'Queen of hearts.' A smile spread across his face. 'A very suitable card don't you think considering we are playing for a woman.'

Ariel gave no indication as to how he felt about his defeat. They were brothers and although there was rivalry between them there was also affection. Slowly, Ariel smiled too.

'This is too easy,' he said, and shook his head as he settled himself more comfortably. 'We've done this before, betting as to who gets her into bed first.'

Aristo shrugged. 'What else do you suggest?'

As the train began moving out of the station, Ariel settled his dark eyes on the passing scene as he contemplated their wager from a different angle.

'Let us,' he said at last, 'wager against ourselves. Let us see who can resist her charms the longest.'

For a moment Aristo stared at his brother as if he were mad. Then they both began to smile and then to laugh.

'Like celibate priests,' joked Aristo.

'Or eunuchs,' returned Ariel and slapped his thigh muscles which bulged thick and hard beneath the creamy softness of his flannel trousers.

Chapter 5

Hearing no reply from within, Andre Lefevre, cabin attendant on the most exclusive train in the world, knocked once more on cabin number three on coach 4302 which was named Ione.

Receiving no reply, he assumed the cabin was empty and pushed open the door. What he saw there stopped him in his tracks.

Over a period of years he had become accustomed to catching the rich and famous indulging in their most carnal desires. But still his mouth dropped open when he saw the two women, one only half dressed, embracing as only a man and a woman should embrace. He gawped before collecting himself and finding his voice.

'*Pardonnez*, mesdames.'

With instant abruptness, he put down the last of their luggage, respectfully lowered his eyes, and quickly departed.

'I think we've shocked him,' mused Virginia, her fingers tracing affectionate lines over Raymonde's face. She wore only her shift, one strap halfway down her arm, one pretty breast exposed. Her belly was pressed tight against that of her lover who was still wearing a dark silk dress and a black wig that was streaked with a few strands of grey.

He groaned once the door had closed and the porter departed. 'Oh, Lord! How will I look that guy in the face when I bump into him again?'

His hand had been on Virginia's breast. The intrusion of

the porter had caused it to loosen. Virginia covered it with her own and encouraged him to squeeze it again.

'Darling. What can he think? That you are . . . shall we say . . . left wing? Limp wristed? Not all man because you are dressed in women's clothes? Silly boy! You, who are every inch a lady's perfect companion with your prim dress and your neat hairstyle? He will never guess you are a man. Never.'

Raymonde sighed and relaxed. He rested his forehead against hers. 'Of course. Seeing two men together is one thing. Seeing two women . . . well . . . I suppose it's different.'

'Of course it's different. Why, I could tell you some stories about the girls' school I went to just after the Great War that would make your hair stand on end . . . or at least . . .' she went on in a lower, more seductive voice ' . . . make your cock stand to instant attention.'

Her voice and her words had the desired effect. Raymonde hugged her closer and murmured his desire against her ear. 'You don't need to do that,' he whispered. 'Just feeling your body against mine is enough to make me hard and hot for you.'

He squeezed her exposed breast until she voiced a pleasurable whimper. At the same time, he slid the other thin strap off her shoulder so that her shift floated to her waist and then to the floor. Only her silk knickers and stockings remained. Her knickers were icy blue and trimmed with satin. Her stockings were silk, flesh-coloured and held up with blue satin garters. As her body moved against him, the silk rustled like crisp leaves running before an autumn breeze.

'I love the sound of silk,' said Raymonde between her kisses. 'I love the feel of it too.' His hands slid to her hips. 'But not as much as I love the feel of your skin.' Her hips swayed gently as his fingers undid the buttons of the fragile garment.

For a moment the delicate item of underwear caught on her garters. Raymonde kicked off the court shoes he was wearing before falling to his knees and disentangling the knickers from her garters. With trembling fingers, he slid them over the firm contours of her thighs. He caused them to linger a while, kissed the front of her knees and stroked the back of them. Once he had finished doing that, he pulled the silk garment down over her calves and down to her ankles.

Her body swayed as she lifted each foot to facilitate the knickers being discarded altogether. As she did this, Raymonde breathed in the scent of her sex, the warm sweetness of her inner thighs.

Groaning with pleasure, he gently gripped her thighs, his thumbs caressing their satin softness. Then, closing his eyes, he leaned forward and buried his nose in her pubic hair. Even with his eyes closed, he could still see her in his mind. The scent of a beautiful woman was in his head. It was as powerful as some exotic opiate, a trigger to his hormones and his passion.

As he moaned softly and rubbed his nose in her hair, his tongue flicked at her sex. Above him, Virginia groaned and slowly opened her legs.

'That is so delicious,' she murmured. 'Never has a tongue given me such delight as yours is giving me now.'

Raymonde did not answer. He was drunk with the scent of her, and still his mouth sucked at her secret lips as if he would have more of her essence.

'Please,' Virginia murmured, her fingers tousling his hair and intermittently gripping at his shoulders. 'Please stop. I don't want to finish this yet. I want to go on. I want to do more.'

Responding to her request, Raymonde's mouth left her sex. He looked up at her over the flatness of her belly and the rise of her breasts. He could see her face, her parted lips, through the valley between.

Slowly, very slowly, he rose and, as he did so, his hands caressed her thighs, her hips, her waist, then her arms. It was as if he were tracing the perfection of her body, the youthful hills and valleys of her flesh. At the same time, his lips kissed her belly and her breasts, his tongue teasing her nipples until they were hard as dried peas. Finally, he pressed his mouth against hers.

'I must have you,' Virginia breathed against him. 'I must have your body!' Her pelvis pulsed against him.

'It's yours.'

Dizzy with desire, Raymonde continued to kiss her face and caress her body. He was aware that as he did so, Virginia's quick fingers were unbuttoning the silk dress he wore. Eventually, it tumbled to the ground in a breathless hush and was followed by the silk underwear she had chosen for him.

He wore no panties. Virginia had insisted on that.

'I will adore thinking of the chill air circulating around your cock,' she had said to him. 'And, besides, think of how much easier it will be to get at.'

The prospect had thrilled him. So had the actuality. He had stood on the station wondering what people would think if they knew that the angular woman with the well-muscled legs and broad shoulders wore no knickers. He also wondered at their surprise if they discovered what was hanging between his legs and what rose so stiffly from his nest of pubic hair.

And now, here he was standing before her, dressed, as she was, in a pair of flesh-coloured stockings held up by a pair of garters. The only difference was that her garters were blue and his were green – and where there was only a patch of pubic hair showing between her thighs, an erect penis rose from between his. It was hard, demanding, and the way it pulsed sent aches of desire up into his groin.

'Look,' said Virginia suddenly, pointing to the mirror. 'See what a sight we are!'

They both began to giggle, then sway together. Raymonde's penis was tight against her belly, his hands spread on each buttock.

Still clinging to her, he ran his fingers down her thigh to the back of her knee. Yielding to his pressure, she raised her stockinged leg, bent her knee and folded it around his thigh.

Raymonde stood with legs apart and buckled slightly so that his penis could easily delve into the moist folds of her sex. As they kissed, both glanced towards the mirror to see the effect they were having.

With his free hand, Raymonde gripped Virginia's bottom, steadied her, then slid his length into her vagina, ably assisted by the flow of her sexual juices.

'We look like some kind of dancing monster,' giggled Virginia against his ear.

'If that's so,' breathed Raymonde, 'then this dance sure beats the Charleston any day!'

Virginia hugged him to her.

'I love your back,' she murmured as she ran her hands over the firm muscles that padded his shoulders and followed the curve of his spine. 'And I love your bottom,' she added as she spread her palms over the tightness of his buttocks.

When their lips were close again, she poked her tongue into his mouth until it met the tip of his. He sucked on it as if he would feed or drink on it.

'But most of all,' she murmured once her tongue was back in her own mouth, 'most of all, I love your cock and I want to feel what it is doing.'

Raymonde gasped, then groaned with pleasure as her hands slid slowly down between their bodies until her fingertips were touching his iron-hard erection.

'I can feel your cock,' she said softly. 'Are my fingers making it bigger?'

'Yes!' he murmured.

'I can feel your pubic hair. Though it might be mine. I'm not sure. It's all getting tangled up together.' She laughed and, breathless with a fresh flood of arousal, Raymonde tried to kiss her lips. She moved her head.

'Let me go in with it. Let my finger go in with it.'

Raymonde stared into her eyes. They were brilliant with lust, sparkling with desire.

Virginia did not wait for him to say anything, to agree or disagree. The index finger of her right hand joined with his thrusting cock and, as her own body juices flooded over them both, her finger and his penis completely filled her vagina.

Raymonde closed his eyes and groaned, a kind of regretful noise because the end of his pleasure was near and he did not want it to end.

Virginia felt as if she was flying like a bird, or one of those new fangled aeroplanes or airships but without any engine. Noiseless, she was soaring on her own wings of delight.

When the high point of their lovemaking came at last, they clung together, their breath racing almost in unison. Only when the last echoes of their pleasure had finally been exhausted did her raised leg return to the floor and his penis slide out of her.

Virginia turned away.

'Run my bath, darling,' she called over her shoulder.

Raymonde frowned. True he had provided additional "services" for rich female guests at the hotels he had worked at in Paris, but he no longer counted Virginia as one of those women. Already he was feeling something more for her. There was a closeness between them that was not just physical. Or at least, that was what *he* assumed. But what about her? From the tone of her voice he was the servant again.

'Then be that,' he told himself. 'Be her servant, her travelling companion. Who knows where it might lead.'

'You had better bathe and change too,' Virginia added as she pulled off her stockings and reached for a black satin kimono. 'Then we shall make our way to the dining car, and from there, my darling Dorothy, I will choose the man I think best suits my needs.'

Chapter 6

The Honourable Davis Sedglingham was admiring his reflection while his valet brushed at the shoulders of his dinner jacket. He straightened and smiled because he very much liked what he saw.

His shoulders were broad but not vulgar in the way that a man that digs roads for a living might ripple with muscle. His limbs were well proportioned, firm yet not uncouth.

If clothes maketh the man, then Davis Sedglingham most definitely was made. There was an impeccable cut to his clothes, a clean-living smoothness to his hair and his chin. Both were taken care of by his valet, Mario. Mario the meek. Mario the self-sacrificing; the much abused.

For all Davis cared, Mario might just as well have not been there at all. He gave him as little regard as a piece of luggage, or the pillow that travelled with him everywhere he went. Davis liked to have familiar things when he travelled, and both the pillow and his valet were pummelled on occasion, the pillow before he lay his head on it, and his valet when the mood took him.

At the moment Mario was a nonexistent item. Davis preened before the mirror as if he were the only man in the room.

'I look a gentleman,' Davis thought to himself as he twisted and turned so he could examine his impact from all angles. 'I look an exceedingly good catch for some unsuspecting young woman with firm breasts, a hot pussy and a hotter bank account.'

As he studied his fair complexion, swept-back hair and the fine line of moustache that adorned his upper lip, Davis straightened his shoulders and raised his hands to adjust his bow tie. As he did so, he inadvertently knocked the clothes brush out of his valet's hand and sent it flying towards the mirror.

As he watched, the reflection he had so admired broke into ugly fragments, a spider's web of cracks in the shiny glass.

The proud countenance that had surveyed the reflection broke in a similar way and rage replaced smugness. There was a twitch beneath his right eye, a certain curling of the lip on that same side. He hissed like a kettle letting off steam before he shouted.

'What clumsy fool do I have here!' He raised his arm.

There was a cracking sound as one man's palm met another's head. Mario, gentleman's valet, went flying and ended up sprawled on the floor.

The valet curled himself up like an unborn foetus. His arm went over his head. Partially shielded by its dubious cover, he peered at the towering Davis whose smooth expression was now creased with anger.

'Look what I have to put up with! Look at this idiot who professes to be a valet.'

Mario said nothing. His frightened eyes just stared from over the top of his arm. Experience had taught him that he was expected to say nothing, to give no defence, not to address his master unless invited to. After all, his master never truly addressed him. He spoke of him as a third person, an entity who might as well not have been there.

'See what responsibilities I have? How many more times do I have to resort to employing some discipline in my life?'

It never occurred to Davis that the discipline he was employing was directed at someone else rather than himself, that he never chastised himself.

He was like some medieval prince for whom a whipping boy is employed to take the punishment that he himself has earned.

Eyes blazing and mouth grim, Davis bent to pick up the clothes brush.

'I'll teach you,' he snarled.

With each footstep that crushed the rose blush of the carpet, the valet closed his eyes a little more tightly and retreated to the place he always went to when his master was angry.

He thought of his boyhood, a time when he had been very happy. He always went there in his mind when his master was beating him. It was the only way he could cope with the blows that fell on his body. The only way he wouldn't lose his job.

Blow after blow thudded across his back and his shoulders. He protected his head with his arms and in his mind he was somewhere else. In his mind he was once more a carefree youth, a dark-haired Romeo. Beautiful girls flashed their eyes at him, sashayed more provocatively than they should have done. Reprimand came from parents and priest, but still the girls would fall for his looks and his words of love.

He had loved all that attention, but one girl alone had taken his breath away.

In his mind the hot sun of August was upon his back as he toiled in his father's vineyard and exchanged smouldering looks with the long-legged Gina. In his mind it was always summer, always the vineyard, and there was always Gina with her big blue eyes and hair that was fairer than anyone else.

Their lust for each other had been irresistible, as hot as the Umbrian sun. People had begun to talk. Jealousies had been ignited. They had resorted to meeting in the vineyard at night, lying naked in the grass and making love beneath the cobweb light of a clouded moon.

No matter what was happening to his body in reality, in his mind his flesh was against that of his love, and his hips jerked in time and in ecstasy with hers.

So intensely real was his memory, that he was hardly aware of the ceasing of the blows. Hardly aware of his master's dissipating violence. He heard only the last trembling anger in his voice.

'You see? This is what I have to do to get things done properly. It is obviously my lot in life to correct those who do wrong, to train a carthorse to be a thoroughbred, a nigh impossible task. My valet is a clumsy man. All servants are clumsy in fact. Calibre has decreased since the war. That's because there are no English valets, you see. I have to resort to foreigners. Dirty, disgusting, stupid foreigners!'

Davis Sedglingham took a deep breath and flung the clothes brush to the floor. Then he straightened his bow tie and smoothed his hair. He did not exit his cabin until he had taken a few more breaths and the pinkness of his face had completely disappeared.

'Right,' he said to himself at last. 'Thanks to my valet I am a little late for dinner. But I'm all ready now.'

Before he left, Davis Sedlingham looked down with contempt on his curled-up servant, then he sniffed and aimed one last kick at the man's backside.

'Foreigners,' he growled as he opened the door himself and departed.

Even after the door had closed, Mario lay still on the floor, his arms hugging his aches and his throbbings. Not one whimper did he utter. A lone tear was not shed for the aching of his body, though, of course, he was black and blue from the beating. The only ache he was experiencing was in his heart. He was no longer a youth and the beautiful Gina now lay with another man. But he had seen someone like her on the train. She too was with another man, an American. He had also seen the look in her eyes and knew she was just as unhappy as he was.

Chapter 7

The dining car was named *Voiture Chinoise* on account of the black lacquer panels imprinted with daintily etched scenes of pagodas, trees, animals, birds and flowers. Despite being black, the panels were bright, rich with soft greens, stark whites, yellow and orange. Reflected daylight coming through the carriage windows gave the birds flight, the animals movement, and the flowers looked to be nodding in a passing breeze.

Dining chairs were capacious, perhaps to allow for the large bottoms of those people who indulged themselves too freely in the wealth created by the labour of more lowly souls.

Rich brocade curtains tied back with silk cords hung at the windows framing the passing scenes as though they were no more than moving pictures for a select Parisienne salon. Glass wall lights shaped like spring tulips gave added richness to the red ochre and creamy beige of the plush upholstery and deep-pile carpet.

Rich aromas of fresh coffee, delicious food and expensive perfume added something indefinable to the atmosphere that was like seasoning to sensuality, or an aperitif to the sexual games that were soon to be played.

Tinkling glass, silverware and fine porcelain added a gentle accompaniment and pink-shaded brass lamps set on each table flushed the face of each diner no matter their age or their pallor.

Waiters, their voices and countenance subdued, glided

between tables, eyes and ears constantly alert to whatever their wealthy diners might need.

Virginia and her companion, "Dorothy", had already ordered from a menu offering *La Fricassée d'Ecrevisses et de Langoustines au Caviar servie dans son Marmiton*.

'It reads like a song. Don't you think?' Virginia said to Dorothy. Her companion merely grimaced as a wicked smile played around Virginia's mouth.

'Don't frown like that, darling,' said Virginia, her hand trailing across her companion's face. Her voice became as soft as her fingers. 'You'll get wrinkles very quickly if you keep doing that. Now what woman in her right mind would want that, darling?'

She raised her hand in front of her mouth to hide her sudden burst of laughter. As she did so, her eyes flashed and took in the details of the other diners. So far, the only ones of interest that were already seated were the two Greeks. To her great disappointment, they merely nodded politely in her direction then turned back to their food.

Maintaining her smile, Virginia watched red wine cascade into her glass. Once that was done, the open bottle hovered over her companion's glass. The waiter looked to Virginia for permission to fill the glass of the "woman" who was supposedly her paid companion, and thus her servant.

Virginia smiled. A wicked pleasure danced in her bright blue eyes. 'Just half for my companion, if you please. She really hasn't got a head for strong spirits, poor dear.'

Raymonde shot her a fierce look. Virginia merely smiled, her eyes tilting at the corners. In that moment, it could almost be imagined she had stepped from the Chinese panels that lined the walls.

The waiter bowed before moving away.

'Now, now, my dear Dorothy.' Virginia raised her voice once the waiter was out of earshot. Her tone was borrowed from the woman she had once worked for, the woman whose husband had become her lover. 'A woman of genteel

48

background should not be seen drinking too much wine. It does nothing but harm to her image. It inflames the blood. Gives rise to lurid thoughts! We can't be having that, can we?' She patted his hand and lifted her glass to her ripe, luscious lips.

Raymonde grimaced. 'So what? It feels great in my throat. And what's wrong with hot blood and lurid thoughts?'

Virginia shot him a warning look and murmured a hushed rebuke. Raymonde had responded a little too gruffly for a servant – and a female one at that.

He shifted in his seat and fidgeted with his clothes. Virginia shook her head reproachfully.

'I can't help it,' he whispered.

He was telling the truth. He could cope with being a waiter, a servant to those of higher class and income than himself. Being a woman he found much more difficult.

'My garters are itching and my feet are aching,' he muttered.

Virginia's bright blue eyes twinkled with delight. 'Stop complaining. Now you know what us women have to put up with all the time. I wish I could be like you and wear trousers as a matter of habit.'

'I've no objection to that and, anyway, at least you're wearing a pair of very silky camiknickers, if I remember rightly. Think of me. At your insistence, I'm wearing none. My balls are hanging free and half frozen.'

Virginia giggled and, if it were possible, her eyes seemed to sparkle even more than they usually did.

'Darling,' she purred, covering his hand with her own and leaning closer to him so that her perfume filled his head and made his naked penis leap between his thighs. 'It excites me to think that you're not wearing any underwear. It's all part of the adventure, don't you see? Imagine what these people would think if they knew what was hanging beneath that matronly skirt!'

A gleam made her eyes shine, which in turn made her face glow as she shifted in her seat. Her eyes seemed to hold his, and he wondered if she was imagining him naked beneath his clothing, just as he was doing. In a way, his wondering was confirmed.

Raymonde gasped as the toes of her stockinged foot edged up under the silk skirt he wore. He gulped on a mouthful of wine as the foot edged onwards and caressed the nakedness of his inner thighs. His penis stiffened as he opened his legs to let her in.

Virginia blushed with pleasure. Her hand covered her mouth in an effort to stifle her giggle. One hand held the glass of wine. The other slid the tip of her cigarette holder between her parted lips.

'Light me up,' she murmured, the tone of her voice adding a seductive dimension to what she was actually saying and what she was actually doing.

As Raymonde responded, he looked directly into her eyes and tried his best to read her thoughts, to understand what made her tick and what she had planned for this trip and for him. At the same time, he did his best to enjoy what was happening without crying out loud. It was not easy. He could barely breathe. What she was doing to him beneath the table was so delicious, so exquisitely wanton. And all the while, other people – rich people – ate quail and drank champagne, talked and sometimes glanced admiringly in their direction. Not one of them could see what was going on and, hopefully, not one of them would guess. He sighed with pleasure. If this was decadence, he wanted more of it.

Virginia's eyes suddenly left his. She was looking beyond his shoulder. He knew immediately that someone had entered the dining car, someone who interested her.

'This way, Lord Sedglingham,' he heard a waiter say with humble servility.

Raymonde willed Sedglingham to correct the waiter's term of address. He himself knew full well that

Sedglingham was only an honourable. But Sedglingham did no such thing and Raymonde was in no fit state to shout it out.

Still gritting his teeth to stop from moaning with pleasure, he glanced over his shoulder.

Impeccably dressed and unbearably handsome, Davis Sedglingham was smiling and heading their way.

Why now? was the cry that echoed in Raymonde's brain. Why now, when Virginia's toes were urging his semen to course through his penis like hot lava from a newly born volcano.

He saw her smile at the ill-mannered man whom he had met – or rather served – back at the George V.

'He's a lounge lizard,' he managed to mutter. He got a quick jab in the testes for his trouble. Virginia's smile was still fixed on Sedglingham. Her foot was still doing delicious things between his legs and Raymonde was willing her to take his erection to its full conclusion. It wouldn't happen if Sedglingham got to their table too quickly.

Slower, Raymonde demanded, move slower!

He almost held his breath as Sedglingham advanced along the carriage. Just a little more time and the fluid surging up through his penis would erupt and spray like hot wax over Virginia's pretty foot.

Inch by painful inch, his semen rose. So great was his need to ejaculate before Sedglingham got there that he held his breath. Just as the first droplet seeped over his crown, Virginia let her foot slide back into her shoe.

Inwardly, he groaned. If there had been no one else around he would have pleaded with her to recommence her ministrations. His body was trembling in that terrible suspense between desire and fulfilment. His penis was still hard, his blood still hot. Yet he could do nothing. He had no alternative but to bring himself under control and content himself merely with looking at her and thinking on what might have been and what might yet be.

51

The thought that he should peer beneath the table just to see her legs also occurred to him.

Virginia chose that exact moment to drop her napkin. Her eyes were fixed on Davis Sedglingham.

'Oh, I'm sorry,' she purred as Sedglingham smiled, bowed and bent down to pick it up. 'What a clumsy fool I am.'

Slippery as spilt olive oil, Sedglingham's smile spread across his too-wide mouth. Raymonde wondered what those thick lips would feel like against his fist. He didn't know quite why he thought that. Perhaps it was because Sedglingham's appearance had curtailed his climax. But he didn't think so. It was just that he struck Raymonde as a man who deserved to be punched and who had so far been lucky not to have been.

With sinking heart, he listened to what he considered to be mindless banter between them.

'Clumsy? That is is the last word I would use to describe you, mademoiselle. Even though I do not know your name, I would still be so bold as to call you graceful more so than clumsy.'

Raymonde saw their fingers touch as Davis passed the napkin back into her hand. Such a light touch, yet heavy with intent. He imagined the tingle of aroused sensuality running like electricity between them.

The errant honourable did not even glance at the un-gainly "woman" who sat frowning on the other side of the table, looking on him without one ounce of welcome. His attention was strictly focused on his prey.

'Please allow me to introduce myself. Davis Sedglingham. My card, mademoiselle.'

Again their fingers touched. Raymonde saw his new mistress turn a subtle shade of pink. He wondered if that pinkness had spread all over her skin and wished he was the man who might follow its course.

Virginia put every bit of sensuality she had into that

smile. 'Virginia Vernon. This is my travelling companion Dorothy Plumber. She goes everywhere with me.'

Davis barely glanced at Raymonde. Just the briefest of nods. His gaze remained fixed on Virginia. 'Everywhere?' Davis lifted his brows. 'Isn't that dependent on what you are doing; who you are with?' A raised eyebrow and a lopsided smile hinted at sexual connotation.

The smile Virginia gave him in return was serene and, if it could be possible, even more suggestive than his had been. 'Everywhere, my lord,' she said, her voice oozing seduction. 'Absolutely everywhere.'

Her eyes held his. His thin lips continued their salacious smile, but Virginia did not let herself analyse that smile. 'He desires me,' she told herself. 'He's stripping me naked with his eyes and his mouth is ahead of him, tasting my body, sucking my breasts.' She shifted in her seat as she felt that old familiar tingle at the top of her legs. It made her want to sigh. It made her want to groan. For the moment she saw only him. Even the question of his wealth did not enter her mind. For the present, his body was enough.

Raymonde felt awkward and tried to look everywhere but at them. He did not need to see them doing anything sexual. The electricity of attraction was there. In his mind he could imagine his lordship stripping off her clothes and spreading her legs. Instead of Raymonde's mouth licking at her curly forest of pubic hair, tasting the sweetness of her sex upon his tongue, it would be Lord Sedglingham. Raymonde could see it all clearly. The look was there in the man's eyes. Raymonde could read his mind. It made him feel like a voyeur.

'Davis. Please call me Davis,' Sedlingham was saying. His voice had become a rich purr. Not like that of a cat, more like a predatory panther. 'Perhaps you could join me for dinner,' he went on. 'I'm sure your companion can look after herself.'

The shoulder strap of Virginia's silver silk dress slipped off her shoulder and exposed a few extra inches of soft, white flesh. She made no attempt to retrieve it.

'How delightful,' Virginia purred, and Raymonde thought how long her neck was, how tight the pearl and silver ribbon of her choker.

Virginia looked directly at Raymonde and there was no disguising the gleam of excitement in her eyes. 'Dorothy is a big enough girl to look after herself. Aren't you, Dorothy darling?' Now it was Virginia's turn to look like a cat. Still gleaming, her eyes again tilted ever so slightly upwards at the corners so that they looked like elongated almonds. Her smile was wide and had a hint of deviousness about it.

Raymonde, unsure of quite what to do next, nodded and muttered a muted acquiescence. Silently, his eyes followed as Sedlingham helped Virginia from her seat, one arm around her waist to help guide her to a spot where he could seduce her in private.

Raymonde swallowed his jealousy. Eyes wide and brain racing, he considered all the things they might talk about, all the things they might do together.

'Slut,' he muttered. As if it might drown his feelings, he gulped the last of his wine and stared out of the window.

France lay sleeping, the blackness of the night relieved only by the odd square of light shining from a farmhouse window or a chateau perched high upon an ebony hill.

Reflections of the diners and waiters moved over the window pane; muted shapes and colours of the world within reflected on the blackness of the world outside.

One particular shape loomed larger. Raymonde became aware that someone was waiting to speak to him.

'Madam?' The word was pronounced precisely, but with caution. There was a hint of East European, possibly Balkan, about the accent.

Raymonde turned round and looked into the face of a man named Zweizer. He remembered him from the guest list at the hotel. The man was a banker: one of the celebrated Gnomes of Zurich. He remembered him having a wife who spoke in a constant monotone and was lofty in height and manner.

'I am sorry to interrupt your thoughts, madam, but I wonder if I might make your acquaintance.' His voice was breathless, as though he had just run up a rather steep flight of stairs.

'I don't . . .' Raymonde began, afraid that he might have aroused the man's hormones dressed as he presently was.

Without waiting for any encouragement, the banker slid into the seat opposite. His fat fingers interlocked on the table between the cutlery placement before he spoke. He leaned forward, his voice low but still breathless. His tongue flicked out every few words.

'Dear lady. Please do not be alarmed. My name is Heinrich Zweizer. I am travelling with my wife. It is our thirtieth wedding anniversary, you understand. This is our celebration. Our second honeymoon if you like.'

His laugh was hollow and there was a pained look in his eyes. Thirty years of hell or monotony? Raymonde wondered.

'I . . . uh . . .' Raymonde pulled himself up. His voice was a touch too deep. 'You're pretending to be a woman,' he reminded himself. He pitched it a bit higher. 'My name's Dorothy . . .' He paused as he tried to remember what surname Virginia had used. What the bloody hell was it? 'Carpenter! Dorothy Carpenter,' he blurted, then realised he'd done it wrong. 'Wrong trade,' he thought to himself. 'Oh, shit!'

'Nice to meet you Madam Carpenter.'

Raymonde ignored the proffered hand and kept his clasped together in his lap. There was no way he was having another man kiss it. There was also no way that Zweizer wouldn't feel the dark hairs that pushed through his skin. He would immediately guess that Dorothy was not only no lady, she was no woman either!

Raymonde drew his knees together; purely a reflex action. What erection remained lessened as his balls bunched back into his body.

'Nice to meet you, Herr Zweizer.' Raymonde nodded his head and managed to smile – just enough to cover his deceptive appearance.

Zweizer licked his lips and leaned closer. 'I hope you do not mind me asking, but I wanted to know about your mistress.' He paused and Raymonde detected lust in his eyes. 'I understand that Miss Virginia Vernon is a lady of some standing in London society. My wife would be very interested in hearing about London society. We would very much like to get to know people in such circles when we are next there. I am sure my wife would be very pleased if I went to her with some contacts in London. Do you think Miss Vernon would oblige me?'

Raymonde studied the beady eyes, the bald pate and the overall picture of a rich, but ugly man. At a rough guess it wasn't London society that Zweizer wanted Virginia to oblige him with.

'I could ask her,' Raymonde offered helpfully, slightly relieved that Zweizer wasn't after his body. 'I could get her to write some names down and she could meet your wife tomorrow perhaps. Would that be . . . alright?'

Zweizer did not appear to notice Raymonde's momentary lapse into everyday American slang. There were other more carnal considerations on his mind. He leaned a little nearer until the smell of his cologne made Raymonde's nostrils quiver.

A fat, wet tongue licked over ripe lips. 'No. No. I do not think you quite understand. I would like to speak to Miss Vernon alone. I want this to be a complete surprise to my wife.'

A slow smile crossed Raymonde's face. 'I bet . . .' he began, then corrected himself. 'I expect you do.'

'I would make it worth your while,' Zweizer repeated, his voice low and laced with the heat of sexual intent.

Raymonde watched the slow progress of Zweizer's hand as it disappeared beneath the lapel of his dark blue jacket. The jacked opened slightly to reveal the deep purple of a satin lining. Raymonde also glimpsed an inside pocket from which a wad of what looked to be notes protruded.

Zweizer flicked them with his fingers as he might a deck of cards. 'When I say I will make it worth your while, I really mean it.' He smiled.

Raymonde couldn't help looking. There was more in that guy's pocket than he could ever hope to make in a year. He also couldn't help thinking what guy wouldn't consider selling out his best friend when faced with a wad of notes like that? Virginia was adorable, but she was also his employer. He was merely her servant. What chance did he have to win her permanent affection?

He cleared his throat. 'I'll see what I can do.'

Zweizer, his smile fixed as though it had been painted on, nodded his head gratefully. 'That will be very good. Very good indeed.'

The man's smile reminded Raymonde of the sort favoured by circus clowns, and the man was a clown alright. 'What fools we men are,' he thought to himslf. 'All clowns together,' he mumbled once Zweizer had gone.

Ariel and Aristo Kostopoles grinned at each other, their rings flashing as their hands brought their food up to their mouths. Aristo spoke first.

'He's got there before us. Our wager is now pointless.'

Ariel shook his head, his lips wet with the wine he had just sipped. 'It won't last. From what I know of that Englishman, he has more of an appreciation for money than for women. Still,' he said with a smile, 'it does help us curtail our passion, does it not?'

Aristo sighed and pressed his hand into his groin. 'But not easily. Did we truly agree on a wager of fifty thousand dollars?'

Ariel smiled as he sat more comfortably in his chair and brought his wine to his lips. 'We did.' He drew on a large cigar and held his head to one side. There was a thoughtful look on his face. 'Interesting, don't you think. We are weighing up which we value the most.'

Like the Englishman, thought Aristo as he smiled at his brother, and he wondered how he could both seduce Virginia Vernon and also win the wager.

Chapter 8

It had excited Virginia to toy with Raymonde's penis in the dining car. Enhanced by imagining how aroused he was feeling, her own desire had spread over her body like a fine cobweb.

Throbbing and hot against the ministrations of her toes, his erection had grown and pushed against the sole of her foot.

Even now she could feel the residue of his warmth and his hardness impressed upon her skin. It was difficult to get his image out of her head and she could not help thinking of how vulnerable he must feel dressed in those matronly clothes, his genitalia hanging naked between his legs. What an ingenious idea it had been to have him not wear any knickers. And him, dear soul, had gone along with it . . . for her sake.

Raymonde was a delight – but now he was out of sight and about to be put out of mind. Her eyes smiled at Davis Sedglingham. 'This,' Virginia told herself, 'is the man you should be concentrating on. He has all the right credentials. He's handsome, rich and titled.' That in itself was enough to arouse her interest, but it didn't stop there. Sexuality was something he wore with as much casual perfection as he did his jacket or his tie. Relaxed as his body and his smile might be, they were meant to tempt, to entice.

She could feel the animal attraction in him. Perhaps it was the way he smiled, the undisguised lust in his eyes. Lust was something she could deal with. Perish the day

59

when no one lusted after her. 'Let me have lust and seduction till the day I die,' she thought to herself. 'And when I am dead, I'll leave an instruction that some lively man with a stiff prick must get in the coffin with me – just to make sure I have truly gone. The mourners will see the reaction pretty quickly if not.'

Looking pleasantly pliant, her eyes took in all she could see of the man sitting opposite her. Any girl would be more than pleased to roll up her skirt and let down her silken underwear for the likes of Davis Sedglingham. But could she control him in the same way she did Raymonde? It was a point waiting to be proven.

Purposely, she dropped her napkin again. It would have been easy to pick it up herself or to call a waiter to do so. But Virginia did neither of those things. Instead she glanced momentarily at it, then slid her eyes upwards to focus on Davis Sedglingham's face. There was no doubting the demand in her expression. Her eyes were wide, her lips almost pouting in a spoilt, wilful way.

For a moment he did nothing. Their eyes met, their wills locked. Then he smiled, bent down, and picked the napkin up.

'Yours,' he said.

'You?' she asked in a honey-brown voice full of sexual promise. 'Or the napkin?'

'Bo . . . th,' he answered, the word drawn out long and low. She could not mistake the passion in his voice.

On the outside, Virginia smiled sweetly. An unladylike whoop of triumph echoed in her brain. This was the first beautiful man she would seduce on this beautiful train. He would not be the only one. She could not stop at seducing just one man. After all, hadn't she promised herself she would try out several likely males before deciding who would provide her meal ticket for the next few years? And anyway, seduction once tasted can become very addictive.

Seduction was only a word to most people. Seduction to

60

Virginia meant enticing, ensnaring, and making the subject act in a way they had never acted before. In short, seduction was the making of a slave. She had already made a slave of Raymonde, but that had been easy. He was merely a waiter, ensnared more so by her beauty than her wealth. If she really thought about it, she could almost believe him in love with her. 'What a sweet thought,' said the more sentimental side of her nature. 'But love doesn't pay the bills, take you to the theatre, to Cannes, or to Nice. Only money can do that.' Davis Sedglingham had both the looks and the wealth. Love didn't come into it, but might grow in time.

'So,' she murmured, smiling sweetly at the confident aspect of the man who sat opposite her. 'Tell me about yourself.'

He sighed, smiled and dropped his voice to a seductive level. 'What can I say that would be of interest to one as beautiful as you?' He shrugged casually, as if the details of who he was and what he owned were insignificant. He took her hand in his. His nose stayed firmly in the air. 'I am titled. I have an old house and older estates which were handed to my family by some grateful old king – the one with the six wives I believe.'

Virginia raised her eyebrows and, half hiding a smile, rested her chin on her hand. 'My word. I wonder what your old ancestor did to gain that?'

Davis shrugged, lit a cigar and helped her to light her cigarette. 'Who knows? Perhaps he helped divest some old abbot of his tithe.'

Amusement on her lips, Virginia raised her eyebrows. 'Or perhaps he had some daughter who was willingly divested of her underwear.'

Davis smirked. 'Would a daughter do that for a father?'

Virginia threw back her head as she laughed. 'Good lord, no. That would be incest. But she might very well do it for a man with a crown or a coronet and a very big codpiece.'

Davis raised his eyebrows in amusement. 'A big codpiece,

eh! My, my Miss Vernon. You certainly are a witty one. You really are.' To Virginia's surprise, he did not laugh. His smile remained fixed, as though permanently carved in his face.

She did not allow herself to dwell on his lack of laughter. He looked amused and that might be enough humour in a man with his wealth. She soldiered on.

'My name's Virginia.' She smiled a sugary smile that a man like him might appreciate. 'Ginny if you prefer. I get better with encouragement, Mister Sedglingham.'

'Lord Sedglingham actually. But do call me Davis.' His hand covered hers. So soft was his palm against her skin, that she did at first have an urge to remove it. But she stopped herself. What had she expected? Hard skin etched into his flesh like potholes etched in rock? This was not a man used to working for a living. This was a man used to having others work for him.

And besides, he was looking into her eyes with obvious passion. 'I will do everything to encourage you, Virginia,' he said. 'Everything and anything, and I'll start with ordering a bottle of cognac. Waiter!' When he had been speaking to Virginia it had been warm, now it became harsh and demanding.

'One moment, monsieur.'

The waiter who had responded was bent over some elderly woman. She was talking avidly against his ear and seemed disinclined to let him go.

Davis glared and half rose from his seat. 'Waiter! Now!'

Demand was a growling anger in his voice. Virginia looked up at him as if she were far more shy than she actually was. But it wasn't shyness she was feeling. 'This is an impatient man,' she thought to herself, 'though I should not judge him too hastily just yet.'

The waiter continued to attend to the clinging woman. Davis continued to drum the table with the fingers of one hand whilst peering angrily at both the woman and the waiter.

This was not quite the sort of behaviour Virginia had either expected or experienced in any wealthy man she had ever met. In an effort to cool his anger, she touched his hand, her fingers caressing his knuckles as she spoke.

'Davis, my dear man. Perhaps you would at least have the courtesy to give me your attention whilst we are waiting. I cannot think that you would waste time getting angry when you have me to help you while away the waiting.'

Her soft words and soft touch had the desired effect.

Davis turned to face her and his expression softened. The still smile returned. A certain hard glitter replaced the coldness that had been in his eyes.

'My dear Virginia, you are so right.' He laid his hand on top of hers. Virginia looked at it and rested hers on top again. Her fingers stroked his. She liked the feel of them, the proportion of the fingers, the slightly furred skin. Unworked hands, she thought to herself. Hands that had never in all their existence had to do anything manual for a living. Something about that irked her, but she set it aside, told herself that this man could make things good for her. Sexually and domestically, he could turn out to be a good thing.

In her mind she rehearsed exactly what she wanted to say so that when she actually spoke she would sound absolutely believable.

Her sigh was soft. Her look was disarming.

'Your skin is so soft. I like the feel of it. I can imagine how your hands would feel on my body.'

She saw his eyes lower and realised he was watching the movement of her lips as she spoke. Could he imagine them doing other things, she wondered? Was he thinking of how they might feel on his body, kissing his chest, his belly, or even . . .

She moved her legs, met his eyes as one stockinged leg rasped against the other as she crossed and uncrossed her legs. She did it again –just for effect.

The look she gave him was pure seduction.

His mouth opened slightly as though he were expelling a particularly deep breath. Either that or his stomach muscles had condensed to almost nothing as his cock sprang away from his body.

Only his eyes betrayed his desire, and Virginia took note of that.

'You haven't answered my question,' she murmured. 'Can you imagine feeling my body? I can very well imagine how your hands would feel. But then, I have a very vivid imagination.'

'I admire your imagination, dear lady,' he murmured. 'But mine, I must admit, is very poor. I do not wish to imagine how it would feel. I need to experience the real thing. I need to feel you. I need to see your naked body. Would you allow me?'

The waiter chose that exact moment to extricate himself from the woman's demands and come to their side. He stood with head slightly bowed.

Virginia held her answer.

'Can I assist monsieur?'

Davis had no anger left in him to hurl at the waiter. He was smiling at Virginia.

Not once did Davis's eyes leave her as he barked out his order. 'Two cognacs. Immediately.'

'*Oui*, Monsieur.'

In her mind, Virginia was assessing this man, weighing up exactly why she was attracted to him. She was also deciding on his suitability as her future benefactor and lover. Of course, she couldn't really decide that just yet – not until she had peeled those well-cut clothes away from his body and sampled his loving technique. She stretched her body. Not a full stretch that included her reaching far above her head, but a kind of rippling, instant wave that ran from her shoulders, through her legs and down to curl her toes. That was how Davis affected her or, maybe, it was purely how sexual thought affected her.

Sexual seduction was her aim and sexual seduction was next on the list.

The cognac was swiftly brought, swiftly drunk – at least by Virginia.

'Thirsty?' asked Davis, surprise written all over his face.

'Ye . . . sss,' she hissed in a low, growly voice, her upturned face moving closer to his. 'Thirsty for you. Hungry to try your body.'

Davis had been holding his own drink just before his lips. The journey to his lips and onto his tongue was taking a lot longer than it should have. Suddenly, as if he had made a momentous decision, he tipped the whole lot into his mouth.

'Do you travel as well as this cognac?' he asked.

She smiled as she raised her eyebrows. 'I remain mellow, seductive to the taste buds as I am sucked in and like fire once I am more fully digested.'

The strained smile which Virginia had quickly come to expect spread over Davis's face. 'I have a preference for indulging my tastes in private. Indeed, I can think of nothing better than being alone in my cabin with an inspiring indulgence, especially one that turns to fire on the tongue.'

Smile still firmly fixed, he rose to his feet and offered her his arm.

For a moment, she hesitated and stared at the arm as if it might sting her. Was she still in control, she asked herself?

The strained smile on Davis's face began to fade. A warning note sounded in her brain. There was no time to consider whether or not she was still the seducer and he the seduced. Her future comfort depended on acquiring the right man for the job. So did the delights of the bedroom.

Chapter 9

Heinrich Zweizer squeezed himself past the brash little American tart. Her brow furrowed as she glared at him over her shoulder. Zweizer only beamed. To his great delight, she did not protest as his belly and his groin pressed against her firm, young body.

'So sorry, madam,' he murmured, his mouth wet and wide as he smiled. It was a lie and there was a definite perversion in telling it.

As his bulk pressed against her, he felt the curve of her bottom against his latent sex. Because his belly had pushed into her back, her buttocks had tilted that much more and were pressed against him. For the briefest of moments his penis stiffened and raised its sleeping head.

Deliciously wicked shivers ran over his stout frame and there was a stirring in his groin, though God knows he had no chance of seeing that article he had used so well in his youth.

But just the firmness of her flesh and the thought that only satin covered her silken skin was enough to set his pulse racing. Zweizer was a man with a very vivid imagination. Besides that he was as dapper in appearance as he was in business. Banking required him to be precise and sharp of mind and perhaps more than a trifle conservative. In dress he was much the same. His collar was stiffened into small wings over his tie. Both trousers and jacket were of a solid colour and he wore white spats over highly polished shoes.

Senses ignited, he swept on, his round face still shiny and merry as an autumn apple. His thumb hung from his waistcoat and his fingers drummed a steady beat against his rotund belly.

Through carriages full of rich people with richer dialects, he wound his merry way, almost oblivious to the chatter of those lounging and being served, the clatter of the busy souls who were only there to be of service.

He sighed happily to himself at the thought of the blonde's body against his, then went into the bar and ordered a large whisky.

Once the spirit had gurgled into the glass, he held it up to the light, eyed its golden hue with an informed eye, then let it stand a while before he took the first sip. Whisky, he knew, should be mused over before being tasted. Whisky, like women, he believed, was something he knew a great deal about.

He had been on a visit to a distillery in Scotland when he had acquired a taste for highland malts and other things Scottish. Whisky was not the only thing he had encountered in that cloudy country where day was long and light in summer, and a near permanent darkness in winter.

As the warm liquid burned the back of his throat and warmed his blood, he allowed the memory of Scotland to resurface. Even now there was a lovely freshness, a much felt freedom about the memory.

Thankfully, Agnetha had not accompanied him on that particular business trip. Boardrooms and chilly Scottish houses were most definitely not her style. She had stayed in London, visiting the theatre and chatting with women of her own standing. They, like her, had husbands who oiled the wheels of industry while their wives rusted at home.

He'd been a bit younger then, but much more virile than he was now, though such a truth was never admitted.

As the second mouthful of malt trickled into his throat, he thought of that Scottish autumn, of the first sprinkling of snow on the purple peaks, and the sight of a woman's white body being offered for his pleasure.

Abigail MacDonald had been bored. Her husband was the man Zweizer had been there to see, a dry man of business like himself, and like Agnetha, his own wife, Abigail's sensuality was surely neglected.

Rather than staying in a hotel whilst he and MacDonald did their business, Zweizer was invited to stay at the MacDonald home, Barbeggie Hall, a castle with steep sides and walls of dark granite.

Generous helpings of fresh game and highland malt had been laced with a warm welcome and weaker men could have easily been encouraged to relax and ignore the reason for being there. But Zweizer had as great a lust for business as for sex. On the morning of the second day he had proclaimed to his host that he had paperwork to do in his room and, whilst the whisky baron went to his office in the town, Zweizer, after consuming a generous breakfast of oats, kippers, eggs, bacon and kidneys, had gone to his room.

The room was round and pleasant. It had three windows that were little more than arrow slits, but each gave a good view of the countryside surrounding Barbeggie Hall. One looked down the valley towards the town and the steaming distillery. The second stared across to the mist-covered mountains, and the third looked out over the private garden. With such views there was little need for pictures on the dark grey walls, so swathes of tartan material were the only decoration.

Besides that, there was a fire in the grate and a silver tray complete with decanter and two or three small tumblers.

Bundling his papers under one arm, he had sat himself down at the heavy old desk that stood in one alcove. Once the roll top had been eased back, he set himself to work, juggling the figures he needed to juggle, adding a plus here, a minus there.

69

Just as he was rubbing the bridge of his nose where the wire of his glasses had turned the skin a trifle red, there was a knock at the door.

Refreshment, he thought. He had eyed the whisky of course, but work beckoned so he had sensibly resisted.

'Come in,' he called as he turned back to his work. The door had slowly opened and a smell resembling burnt heather had come to his nose.

'Mister Zweizer. I've brought you some tea. Do you like tea? I brought you some shortbread too. Do you like shortbread?'

He immediately recognised the voice of his client's wife. He had noticed earlier that her eyes had settled on him in a more than friendly way, but had told himself he must be mistaken. He was tired from too much travelling and too many figures. Now, judging by the look on the woman's face, there was more than a suspicion in his mind that Mrs MacDonald would oblige him with more than just tea given half the chance.

'No, no,' he told himself on studying the high cheekbones, the tilt of her chin and the gleam in her eyes. 'You are merely imagining things.' He collected himself and managed to answer.

'That is very kind of you,' he said in his abruptly pronounced English as he rose from his chair and bowed politely.

'I'll put it here,' said the red-haired Mrs MacDonald, her words as rolling as the hills beyond his window. 'That'll force you to take a break from those figures,' she said. 'And when I think you are ready for me, I'll be back for you.'

He had glanced only briefly at her face. Her words had made him think it wasn't the tray she was referring to when she talked of coming back for him. She was smiling and had a more than merry look in her eye. He'd felt very vulnerable.

'Perhaps,' he'd thought to himself, 'I am merely imagining she is offering me much more than tea. Perhaps these people have got into the habit of appearing warm to make up for living in a very cold place.'

A mound of warm flesh brushed his cheek as she leaned over the desk to set the tray straight.

Was it his imagination, or had she thrust her breast more closely to his face on purpose? And why were her fingers twiddling that knob in the corner of the desk? Was she imagining it might be something else?

Not wishing to appear a fool, he had turned to his tea tray as though he had neither eaten nor drunk for a fortnight.

Mrs MacDonald straightened. 'Well, I'll be seeing you shortly then.' She had paused. 'When you're ready.'

Once she had departed and the door had closed, he had breathed a heavy sigh and slouched in his chair. His mind, which was usually so full of figures, had been in turmoil. The feel of her breast remained like a breath of dew on his cheek and a raging thirst had manifested itself in his loins rather than his throat.

He pushed at the tea tray and, almost as if he wanted to feel whatever she had felt, he touched his cheek. There was a certain warmth there. Had he been imagining things, or had she actually been sending him sexual signals?

His eyes landed on the knob she had touched. He reached for it, twiddled it like she had, then gave a start as a half-hidden flap sprang open.

Tea forgotten, but Mrs MacDonald still in his mind, he reached into the dark aperture.

Half expecting it to spring shut on his fingers, as though it were some trap she'd prepared especially for him, he had proceeded with caution. Rather than any metal device pinning his fingers, he had touched items of stiff paper with shiny surfaces. It was not his desk and not his things in it, but his curiosity was instantly aroused.

71

Pushing the tea tray further aside, he pulled out the items beneath his fingers. Making a bit more room, he lay them out before him.

Astonished at what he saw, his eyes became wide. His jaw became slack. Before him were some of the most lewd photographs he had ever seen. A man of a more puritanical disposition might have thrown them on the fire, or at least returned them to their secret resting place. But Zweizer was not puritanical. One hand went to his chest as if he were trying to soothe the thudding heart that thumped against his ribs. He could not stop staring. Could not possibly put them away.

Seeing one photograph was like taking that first sip of whisky. One sip was never enough. Neither was one moment of looking. He had to look longer; had to devour her with his eyes. That way the image would stay with him. That way, after one sip . . . He attempted to stop, but couldn't. He had to look.

The first photograph was of a woman whose face was hidden from the camera by her raised arm. A swathe of lightweight material circled her body but did not hide her nudity.

A rose peeped from between her toes. Her legs were heavy, though not unpleasantly so. Womanly hips narrowed to a slim waist and breasts that would amply fill a man's hand thrust forward as if begging to be fondled.

Because one leg was raised slightly, most of the woman's pubic hair was hidden. A few stray tufts had been softly shadowed by the process used to develop the black and white photographs that were swiftly replacing those in sepia.

He had decided there and then that the true colour of her pubic forest must be blonde, red, or even light brown. Swallowing a slight gasp, he slid the first photograph to one side.

In the second photograph, the woman was still hiding her face, her gaze turned away from the camera. Her body faced forward, all of it open to his view.

She was sitting on a chair, her body square to the lens that watched her. Her legs were wide open. Zweizer's heart had skipped a beat as he stared at the cluster of light-coloured hair. Had it been his over-zealous imagination, or could he discern the more solid substance of her clitoral flesh?

His hand had trembled. He remembered that clearly and, as he remembered, he half closed his eyes and took another sip of his whisky. Some part of the train carriage he sat in was immediately obliterated from his gaze. Helped by another sip of whisky, he let his mind wander back.

As he considered the subject of the third photograph, he could almost believe that the same sweat he had felt then was breaking out on his forehead, and the same rush of blood was surging through his body.

In the third picture, a figure was standing behind the woman. Judging by the clothes, he was most definitely a man, and judging by what he was doing, he was truly enjoying his job.

His arms were around her shoulders, his hands cupping her breasts and his thumbs next to her nipples.

Mouth agape, breath rushing from his throat, Zweizer had stared.

For a while it had proved almost impossible to let the photograph fall from his hand. For a while he did not want to turn to the fourth photograph. It would have been easy to sit there and stare at the naked woman who was being so pleasantly mauled by a fully dressed man. And, of course, another man had watched. There was a second man behind the camera claiming the occasion for posterity. Zweizer could have gone on drinking in the coolness of her flesh, but the next photograph had beckoned.

The pose in the next shot had taken him by surprise at first. This time the woman's backside was facing the camera. She was bending low so that her beautiful posterior filled the frame.

Zweizer's breath had caught in his throat. Even now he could feel his blood pounding against his temples, his penis hardening some way below his belly.

His eyes had narrowed to fine slits as he peered at the ripe rear and caught sight of her bush peeping through the gap at the top of her legs. He could also just make out the shape of her breasts which rested like ripe grapefruit on the seat of the chair.

He had groaned and let one hand slide to test the hardening mound that pushed against his trousers. The thud, thud, thud of his heart seemed to echo in his head. The heat of his blood seemed to be attempting to pour out of his skin, and his breath was interspersed with small cries of delight.

'Or am I bleeding?' he suddenly asked himself.

With frightened eyes, he studied each of his sweaty palms, but sweat was all he saw. There was no blood. Nothing except the emission of fluid as his temperature rose higher.

Hardly able to stifle a moan, he had shifted a little in his seat. No longer was he so comfortable as he had been. His erection was growing and getting harder. Curiosity was also growing. The fifth photograph had beckoned.

With quaking heart and trembling fingers, he placed number four to one side and took hold of number five. His gasp of surprise and delight had seemed to echo around the room, to bounce off the sombre walls and dance over the red, green, blue and yellow of the adorning tartans.

'Incredible!' he had muttered.

Wet tongue had licked dry lips as his eyes took in the nude figure. Again she had changed pose. In the fifth photograph she was kneeling. Her head was thrown back so that her torso appeared to be thrusting towards the camera. Her arms were stretched above her head, her wrists held

74

by the same man who had held her breasts.

Zweizer had groaned then and he groaned now as he closed his eyes and reinvented the picture he had seen then.

The round breasts, the flat belly and open thighs had looked vulnerable, fit for a man to stroke and pleasure for her satisfaction, but mostly for his own. But the woman's beauty and vulnerability were not the only aids to arousal. This picture had a slight detail added. Resting on the woman's forehead and along her nose was a length of masculine flesh.

The tip of the penis was immediately above her mouth. The woman's lips were pursed. She was kissing it.

For a while, Zweizer had held this last photograph. When he had at last returned it to the viewed pile, the wetness of his finger and thumb print shone on its surface.

'I can't go on like this,' he had said to himself, head back, eyes closed. There was only one more photograph left. Could he look? The lump in his trousers was becoming painful.

Both hands had slid between his legs which he opened a bit wider in order to accommodate the pronounced swelling created between them.

Each fly button was undone and accompanied by a small gasp of pleasure as the pressure on his member was at last released.

Easing his fingers into the opening, he touched the heat of his sex and its hardness surprised him. Never in all his life, neither before marriage nor during, had he ever achieved such an erection.

Groaning with pleasure, he kept his eyes closed as he pulled his penis out into the world. Keeping his fingers folded around it, he slowly opened his eyes and looked down at the sixth and last of the photographs.

This time when he viewed the naked image before him, his penis jumped in his hand and his jaw seemed to fall to his chest.

It was inspiring enough that the woman was bending over, her haunches held tightly by the man behind her, his naked thighs clamped tightly against hers. There was no need for Zweizer to be told that the man's penis was embedded in the woman's body.

Two plump breasts hung like jewels. The woman's hands were tied behind her back. In addition to that, her mouth was full. Perhaps the photographer had become too inspired by his subject matter but, whatever, his trousers were now open and the model's face was pressed tightly against his groin.

All these things, presented in the most graphic detail, were enough by themselves to arouse Zweizer to the highest peaks of sexual pleasure. But there was another, more personal, more pertinent thing that aroused him more. In the sixth photograph he at last saw the face of the naked woman. That woman was Mrs MacDonald.

Just at that sweet stage when he thought his semen would have spurted from his member, the door had reopened.

He heard the door close again; heard the swish of her clothes as she came into the room.

Almost as though he expected pain when he moved, he found it impossible to look round.

In his hand, his penis had pulsed in apprehension of what might happen next.

He trembled as her fingers slid over his shoulders. At last, he opened his eyes.

'Shall we start with the first one?' she had said.

He had not asked her to explain what she meant. He had not even answered her with words. The photographs were the map he was to follow. Picture by picture, Mrs MacDonald had presented him with the blueprint of how she wished their relationship to develop.

Virginia Vernon was nothing like Mrs MacDonald to look at, although she did have that fresh-faced beauty that is assisted by cool breezes and soft rain. 'What chance,' he thought to himself, 'what chance?'

He narrowed his eyes as he downed the last of his malt. Did it really matter if he never got to know her carnally? He could fantasise about her in every city they came to. He was a well-travelled man and knew the right places to go where sexual pleasure was presented as an art and not a sin. Agnetha would not question what he did in each place they visited. His wife would be taken care of on this journey. He had paid Hans well to make sure she was.

The two Greeks bid him goodnight as they passed. He gave them a curt nod. The twins exchanged bemused glances.

'Foreigners,' muttered Zweizer once they were out of earshot. How could he be courteous, he asked himself, with men who did not appear to have any dealings at all with women. They were obviously of other sexual persuasions, he decided, and wondered with a certain amount of disdain whether the two brothers were far closer than brothers should be.

Chapter 10

Whilst Zweizer imbibed his Scottish malt and reminisced on the time he had spent in its country of origin, Davis Sedglingham was guiding Virginia to her cabin. The heat of his palm seeped through her silk dress and made her flesh that much warmer. Modern electric lighting had been turned down to a minimum to conserve the batteries that were slung beneath the belly of the carriage.

The world outside flashed by, an inky sea of blackness dotted only with squares of muted light shed by the passing train.

They had purposely been the last diners to leave the dining car, the last to finish their nightcaps and leave the sumptuous glow of the bar which was situated in the next carriage along.

Even as they ate and drank, their lips, eyes and bodies had flashed easily understood messages. Their tongues talked polite conversation or asked questions about families, places they lived and the world their lives were usually lived in. And yet both spoke words and phrases that appeared to have one meaning, yet might possibly mean something completely different.

Now words had become unnecessary. Both knew what they wanted, and both knew where they were going. As they walked along the creaking corridor, their bodies swayed in time with the travelling train. Every so often Sedglingham's chest would come up against her back; her thigh would brush against him as she reached for his shoulder in order to steady her step.

Virginia half turned as she entered her cabin. She had intended to ask him in as if she were merely inviting him in for a short snifter before bed when, of course, it would not be a drink she would be offering him but herself.

David did not wait for any invitation. He was right in behind her, his body tight up against hers.

As the cabin door closed, Virginia felt his hand tighten on her waist. With a graceful sidestep, she attempted to avoid his touch but failed. Davis held onto her.

Only one small wall light still burned. Too low for socialising, but absolutely right for showing the naked body in the best light possible.

Virginia decided to test him. 'Let me switch on the big light,' she said, but he held her tight.

'No need to,' he murmured as the crispness of his moustache swept across her cheek before he kissed her on the mouth.

Davis was a big man. Tall and lean as he was, Virginia felt half smothered by him and the length of his encircling arms.

Because his hand pressed hard against the hollow of her back, her breasts and belly pressed tightly against him. She could feel a trembling running through his body. She could also feel him hardening against her. This man wanted her sexually. But long term? So far, she could not tell.

'Take it slowly,' she thought to herself. 'Take one step at a time. This is merely step one in my search for a new man, new money and new sex in my life.' His hands ran over her body as if he were moulding her into the sort of woman he wanted her to be.

She moaned with desire, spoke sweet words in his ear and undulated like a sapling tree against him. Her body was on fire.

'This,' she decided, 'is the sort of man and the sort of sex I want!'

The heat of his lips and the smell of his masculinity swept

over her like a shower of light rain. She was drenched in it, tingling with that certain coldness that is a white flame before it burns the flesh.

She murmured deep and low as his hands swept further and encompassed her buttocks, his fingers digging into her flesh, manipulating her body to thrust backwards and forwards against his. She squirmed and whimpered with pleasure as the curve of her mons thudded against the growing hardness in his trousers.

She threw back her head as his lips swept down her neck. Her quickening breath formed into words of exhilaration, delight and demand.

'Darling . . . Don't stop . . . Do it more . . . Kiss me there . . . and there . . . and . . .'

'I'm going to do everything to you,' he exclaimed. 'Everything I've ever wanted to do!'

She did not reply, not in words. She only murmured because it felt as though he were kissing and sucking the words out of her body.

Her breasts tingled. Her nipples hardened. This was the sort of man who could match her own sexuality, she told herself. This man could very well be the one she was looking for.

'Off with your clothes,' he said in a low growl.

With quick, rough movements, her clothes began to slide away. In the dining car, her straps had slid easily from her shoulders. Now they slid further until her dress and underclothes were nothing but a silky cloud around her ankles.

Davis stood at arms' length, his hands gripping her wrists. He stared at her, and although she got the impression he was only studying her from the neck down, she did not let it worry her. When it came to sex, most men could not remember the faces of the women they had slept with. Only the bodies. Only the breasts, the softness or firmness of their bellies or their thighs, the crispness of their pubic hair, and the ease with which they had entered their bodies.

81

So she stood there dressed in nothing but stockings and garters. And yet she tingled beneath his gaze. Her need was so strong. Her sex was bare, damp, and aching with the desire to be touched.

Suddenly, he pulled her roughly to him and his fine clothes were not so smooth now as their crispness rubbed against the softness of her flesh.

'Let me help you undress,' she murmured as she reached for the stiff collar of his dinner shirt.

To her great surprise, he hit her hands away.

For a moment, she didn't know quite what to do, quite what to think. But he did not allow her the luxury of dwelling on her confusion.

He pulled her back to him. His mouth went from her lips, to her ears, to her neck and down to her breasts.

She cried out because his kisses were bruising her flesh, and his teeth as well as his lips sucked too fiercely at her nipples.

'Please,' she pleaded, 'be gentle with me.'

He laughed. It was a sudden, brittle laugh that stopped almost as soon as it had begun. 'I knew you'd say that,' he growled. 'And I know exactly what you mean by it. I know exactly what you want.'

Virginia took a step back. Inside she was telling herself not to panic.

A dark, cruel look came to Davis's eyes. He reached for her, gripped each of her nipples between one finger and thumb of each hand. She cried out as he used her nipples to pull her towards him.

Her breath was suddenly knocked out of her. One arm was around her waist. With his free hand Sedglingham forced her head downwards. At the same time she felt his legs bending as he sat on the arm of a chair.

'Good,' he drawled. 'There's just enough light so I can see your lily white bottom.'

Virginia gasped but willed herself not to cry out. His arm

lay across her back so that she was tightly pinioned across his lap, her breasts trapped between his legs.

'Give me your hands,' he demanded. 'Bring them up behind your back.'

For a moment she hesitated. 'But it's just a game,' she told herself. 'Remember, this is a rich man and perhaps the guardian of your future comfort. Besides, he certainly has the stamina for great sex and it seems he also has some imagination. Who's to say what's to enjoy and what's not?'

There was a sudden sound of ripping silk. Swallowing her reservations, she did as he requested. It was not a big surprise when she felt her wrists being bound – possibly, she thought, with the straps from her dress.

She winced and sucked in her breath. What had been soft silk bit into her flesh as though it had metamorphosed into wire.

'You can struggle if you don't really want to do this,' she thought to herself, and wondered whether that was exactly what Davis wanted her to do. Part of her wanted to protest and shriek that there was something decidedly kinky about his way of making love. The other part of her urged caution. Both were tinged with curiosity and a sense of excitement. 'Relax,' she told herself. 'Think of your future. Look on the positive side. There would never be a dull moment with this man.'

'What an enticing little backside,' she heard Davis say as his hand ran over each buttock in turn, the softness of his palms sending thrills of arousal through her despite the vulnerability of her present situation.

'An enticing little backside and an enticing young woman. A naughty young woman who has been leading me on all night, begging me to do this to her. Begging me to chastise her for being as naughty as she is.'

'Please—' she began.

'Silence! Speak when you are spoken to, woman.'

Panic told Virginia to run. At the same time a mercenary

logic was telling her to stay – so was an odd current of something resembling electricity. Her nerve ends were tingling. Despite her natural fear, there was something inside her that wanted to know how helpless sex might feel.

Whatever Davis had in store for her, she had to endure it. 'After all,' she reminded herself, 'this is only the first man you have tested. He doesn't have to be your final choice. There are many others on this train.'

'How naughty are you, I wonder,' she heard him say. She opened her mouth to answer, then wondered if a response was actually being asked for. As one of his fingers slid down between her buttocks and dipped into her vagina, she decided not.

She tensed as the finger pushed fiercely in but bit her lip to prevent herself from crying out.

'Ah! Just as I thought. Well isn't that typical. Soaking wet, you little whore. I can see I have to put a stop to this, and a little of the sort of discipline I received at school would definitely not come amiss. Now remember. No crying out. No tears. No protests. Is that clear?'

Virginia found her voice. An answer was expected.

'Yes,' she mewed, judging that was the tone of voice he wanted to hear, the sort of voice that made her sound like a frightened kitten.

'Right,' he said. 'Right!'

She felt him fiddling with something and knew instinctively he was getting his cock out.

'What is he going to do?' she asked herself.

The truth came to her when she felt the sticky head of his penis poking against her breast. He wound his arm around her so that his fingers were against her sex. As her clitoris rose excitedly to meet them, she could not help but moan.

Suddenly, the first slap landed on her bare behind. In response, she leapt in his lap, her cheeks rising, but his arm held her tight.

She had a strong urge to cry out as a warm sting spread

over her flesh, but she bit her lip as she remembered the instructions he had given her. She was not allowed to make a sound.

'That,' Davis cried with delight, 'is only the first!'

One slap followed another, and each time she could not help but jolt slightly. The burning of her backside began to intermingle with the teasing ministrations of his finger as her clitoris rose, fat and juicy against it. As her clitoris responded, so did his penis. She could feel it getting wetter and stickier against her trapped breast, could feel it hardening, pulsing against her as his semen travelled up to its summit.

Virginia took deep, sensuous breaths and half closed her eyes as her body responded to the mixture of sexual messages it was getting.

Sensations of pleasure were spreading from her teased clitoris and her beaten behind. There was even pleasure to be had in feeling the tight constraint of his legs against her breasts and the way his penis was beating against them. Added to that, her breasts were aching to be touched as her nipples hardened. The urge to touch them was exceptionally strong, but even that was somehow arousing. She could not touch them herself because her wrists were bound firmly behind her back.

As his fingers manipulated her clitoris, her cheeks got warmer. Cries of delight came into her throat, but were swallowed each time she remembered he had ordered her not to cry out.

Everything about him, about both of them, seemed to be moving in time with each other.

His hand rose and fell on her bare behind, her bottom jolted each time he did it and his penis rammed against her breast and his fingers dabbed against her clitoris.

For a moment she was reminded of a one-man band she had seen in the street, arms and legs all going at once in order to elicit some kind of tune from the instruments he was playing.

On this occasion, she was the instrument being played, an instrument with many parts, many tunes, and all being played and combined by one player.

The tune he was playing was taking her, its rhythm quickening, intensifying until she was completely mesmerised, climbing with its crescendo until the very top note and the fastest tempo had been attained.

Her mouth dropped open, but her eyes closed as her orgasm swept over her.

Suddenly, she cried out as two fingers were thrust rudely into her sex. At the same time, Davis groaned sharply and his semen flowed over her breast, then dripped down her nipple and onto the floor.

He undid her bonds before he left. She had at least expected him to embrace her and kiss her passionately before he went, but he didn't. After untying her, he merely kissed the tip of her nose and held her chin with the fingers of one hand.

'What fun we could have together,' he said with a grin. 'I really do appreciate having someone willing to play the sort of games I like to play.'

After he'd gone, Virginia rubbed thoughtfully at her wrists then called Raymonde from his hiding place.

He was only half dressed – camiknickers and stockings in fact.

Virginia glanced at him but turned away quickly as a flood of instant desire came upon her. Raymonde was not rich. She couldn't possibly . . .

'What did you think of him?' she asked quickly.

Raymonde looked at her intently, then ran his fingers back through his hair so that it lay more flat upon his head.

'A bit demanding for a first date, don't you think?'

Virginia laughed. Inside she wondered whether there was a darker truth in what he had said.

Chapter 11

A brass band wearing dark green uniforms with bright red epaulettes greeted them with a rousing military march at Milan railway station. Or at least, the first impression was that the music was specifically for them. Besides the band, the air was filled with the sound of enthusiasm. If adoration had a smell, it had it here in the pressing crowd gathered at Milan station.

Bunting fluttered in long, crisscrossing ribbons above their heads like brightly coloured birds. Women and children waved little flags, their faces bright with smiles and rosy red cheeks. Both they and the men in the crowd were craning their necks to where a cohort of uniformed men stood in a protective circle around another man. He was making a speech, and in order for his voice to carry and the crowd to see him, he was standing on something that put him head and shoulders above them all.

'I thought they were waving those flags for us,' laughed Virginia, craning her neck in the direction of the cluster of uniforms. 'Who is that little man with the squashed nose and the bald head?'

Raymonde, in his disguise as Dorothy Plumber, craned his neck and looked too. He shook his head. 'Search me.'

Virginia gave him a reproachful look. 'Don't say it like that. It's not ladylike. Besides that, it's very colonial, my dear, and you are supposed to be my genteel travelling companion, not a man from the wild frontier.'

There was no disguising the warning in Virginia's voice.

She fluttered her eyelids before she looked away. Raymonde felt an instant pang of regret that he couldn't see her face. He was growing to love that face, the blue eyes, the high cheekbones, the arched eyebrows that he sometimes thought looked to be in a permanent state of surprise. He even liked her upturned nose, though he would never tell her that her nose was upturned in the first place. Virginia, he had learned, didn't always see herself the way other people saw her.

It was hard not to cup her elbow and steer her through the crowds. Courteous things that only a gentleman would do were things he truly missed when dressed in these lavenders and mauves that Virginia thought suitable for the woman he was pretending to be.

He had asked her why he couldn't dress as a man.

'Are you stupid? How can I catch myself a new lover if it's seen I've already got a young man in tow?'

Raymonde had been disappointed, and not just because he still had to appear to be a woman. He didn't bother to ask her why he couldn't be her lover. He already knew the answer. He had no money and to think on it only made him feel gloomy.

He followed as close as he dared, pushing through where queues of chauffeur-driven cars hired by the more affluent waited to take their passengers into the city. Taxi cabs waited behind them, their blackness glossy with polish. Their drivers were dressed in black caps and jackets in an effort to appear as akin to chauffeurs as was possible. Some were still wiping a rag over the gleaming paintwork and silver bright chrome.

Raymonde noted many a dark-eyed Italian throw an appreciative glance in Virginia's direction as she swept by. Raymonde in turn threw each a warning glare. Today his jealousy was heightened and it was all because of the way Virginia was dressed.

She was wearing a pale green cashmere coat, a gold and

white silk turban and white shoes with contrasting tan inserts. To all intents and purposes, Virginia looked a picture of elegance. But Raymonde knew something the Italian men did not know, and that was what made him feel so edgy. Beneath that coat she wore nothing except her stockings and garters. It was yet another example of the way she treated sex as some kind of adult toy, something to amuse as well as to arouse. What the crowd saw was all that she wore.

'Imagine,' she had laughed, 'what they would think if they knew I am naked.'

'You could get yourself in a lot of trouble,' he had warned, but she had only laughed again. And he had looked at her naked body, wanting it so badly, yet trying hard to restrain himself because if he gave in he would feel as if he were losing some kind of battle.

He had placed the garters on her legs himself. With trembling hands and stilted breath, he had slid them up over the silky softness of her calves, her knees, then her thighs.

His trembling, his breathing and his erection had increased the further up her legs he had travelled. Once the garters were in place, he had gently pushed her knees apart, eased his head forward and, with delicious little kisses, had coaxed her sleeping clitoris into wakefulness.

'That's good,' she had purred, arms braced on the bed, head thrown back. 'Suck me good so that my little button grows and stays tingling. That way, my darling Raymonde, I shall enjoy my little adventure that much more.'

'Imagine,' she had said to him, her voice seeming to melt with delight as she half closed her eyes. 'Imagine all those passers-by pressing against me and the silk lining of my coat rubbing against my skin. And all the time no one will know of how close they are to my body – my naked body.'

He didn't tell her she was repeating herself. He guessed she already knew it and just wanted to indulge herself. She was drowning herself in thinking about it as if she were swimming in a vat of champagne.

Not without jealousy, Raymonde noticed one of the uniformed men give her more than a passing glance. It was almost as though her clothes had suddenly become transparent and the man could see right through to her flesh.

A sense of panic came upon Raymonde. He looked at other men. Were they looking at her in the same way? As though they see the body he had kissed and fondled to arousal this morning?

'Yes,' he told himself. 'Yes!' They were looking at her like that. Even the eyes of the man on the rostrum, who had a bald head and a Roman nose, seemed to follow the elegant form as she swept through the crowd.

'*Bellissima. Bellissima,*' he heard the man in the uniform say before his eyes met Raymonde's.

There was a clicking of heels and a curt nod of the head before the man uttered a word.

'I apologise for my declaration,' he said in impeccable English, hands folded behind his back. 'But your mistress is quite beautiful. It is very hard not to stare at her. Will you tell me who she is?'

Raymonde's mouth dropped open and he looked at the man askance. 'I don't know if I should . . .'

'I think my superior would like to know as well,' he said. His eyes went to the man on the rostrum who was still lecturing the enthralled crowd, his arm rising and falling in tempo with the force of his narrative. His gaze followed Virginia's progress and, although there might have been political fervour in them previously, there was only lust in them now.

'Virginia Vernon,' Raymonde replied quickly, remembering to keep his voice fairly soft and, at the same time, fairly high. 'We're travelling on the Orient Express to Istanbul.'

The man's eyes smiled as warmly as his mouth. 'I will convey this information to Seigneur Mussolini – Il Deuce. I am sure he will be interested. Very interested indeed.'

Raymonde smiled a quick smile. The man in the uniform bowed stiffly then turned away.

'Virginia,' Raymonde hissed as he made good the gap that had sprung open between them. She threw him a quick glance, saw he looked agitated, so she slowed her pace slightly, though not without an air of rancour. 'You've got an instant admirer in Milan,' he said quickly and quietly. 'That guy up there talking to the crowds couldn't take his eyes off you.'

Virginia raised his eyebrows. 'Is he rich?'

Raymonde shrugged. 'I don't know, but he does wear a uniform.'

Virginia shook her head sadly. 'Uniforms are very attractive and are fine for a passing fancy. But that's not why I'm on this trip. Come on. We've got some hunting to do.'

Raymonde did not mention that the man in the uniform had also expressed an interest in her. After all, what little of herself she gave to a man without wealth, she gave to him. He would have liked more, but Virginia had it all set out in her mind what sort of man she was looking for.

'I haven't seen Davis so far today,' he heard her say, and, frowning, she craned her neck and tried to find the tall, fair man among those still descending from the train.

'Make way!' cried one of the blue-coated attendants from the train who was doing his best to break a path for them through the crowd.

Raymonde sighed and wished for the hundredth time he'd been born rich enough for a woman like Virginia. But he hadn't been, so a temporary toy he was destined to remain.

However, unknown to Virginia, he had planted something in Davis Sedglingham's brain that meant she would not be seeing quite so much of him.

Dressed as the too tall, too gawky Dorothy Plumber, Raymonde had been for a cocktail in the bar whilst waiting for Virginia, when Davis had waylaid him. The memory made him clench his jaw. He remembered wanting to take a quick swipe at the man as his fingers had dug into his arm.

'Miss Plumber. How nice to find you alone. Pray come and sit with me and tell me all there is to know about your mistress.'

Raymonde had quelled his need to swing out and slug the guy on the chin. It was then that an idea on how he might keep Davis and Virginia apart had come to mind.

'I believe Miss Vernon has a home in Hampstead,' Davis had began.

Raymonde, as the loyal and humble Dorothy, did not disagree. He didn't add that she also had one in Stepney. Much as he wanted to warn Davis off, to admit to the little he did know of Virginia's background would be much too embarrassing.

He affirmed that what Davis said was correct.

'Such a lucky girl,' Davis extolled, 'being able to survive purely on her own private income. Handed down to her I believe.'

'From an uncle.' It had been stretching a point to call a lover an uncle. Near enough, thought Raymonde.

Davis had looked pleased. He rubbed at his chin whilst he looked up at the ceiling. 'How very nice that Miss Vernon has such true independence.' He had turned to Raymonde then and looked at him very pointedly. 'And tell me, is there any fiancé in tow? Any likely young man that waits for her back in England with his heart on his sleeve?'

'N . . . oo.' Raymonde said it very thoughtfully and really put on an act as though he was having to dredge some secret from his mind. 'But I do believe there is a man in Australia. A sheep farmer I think. Very rich of course. Most of them are, aren't they?'

Davis raised his eyebrows. 'Yes. Yes. I suppose so.' He looked taken aback, but Raymonde judged he hadn't quite given up yet.

With a care not to squeeze his naked balls, Raymonde had crossed his legs so that the silk skirt cooled his thighs and its hem rested gently on his ankles. He clasped his white gloved hands around his knee. He had waited to see what Davis would enquire about next before he put the seed of aversion into his mind.

'And you say she is engaged to this man?' Davis looked almost pale.

'Not quite. I think they have an understanding. Well, he does have the money and Miss Vernon's bank account can't sustain her forever.'

Davis looked askance. It was a while before he put into words exactly what he was thinking.

'Ah. Yes. I see.' He paused, his eyes never leaving the paint and powder that was Raymonde's face for now. 'So Miss Vernon is not an heiress?'

"Dorothy" looked suitably surprised. 'Oh goodness me, no. She is just a wealthy lady who wants to see the world and perhaps get herself a . . .' He had been about to say lover, but stopped himself. 'An education. She never went to finishing school you know. Switzerland has always been very expensive, hasn't it.'

Raymonde judged he had said enough to bring both the conversation and Davis's pursuit of Virginia to a sudden halt. Raymonde congratulated himself on being a pretty good judge of both women and men.

For her part, Virginia was full of apprehension. Davis Sedglingham had indeed made an impression on her – especially on her bottom. It still stung, and that morning, as they had pulled into Milan station, she had viewed it in the mirror. She groaned when she saw it. It still shone with a soft pink glow like a peach that has had a little too much sunshine.

'I shall not be able to sit down all day,' she had said to Raymonde, but he had merely smiled, told her to bend over, then smoothed copious amounts of cooling gel all over her inflamed flesh.

As they exited Milan railway station in a shiny black taxi cab, Virginia left her musing about Davis and their sexual encounter. Anyway, she had experienced serious misgivings about him. It occurred to her that whatever man ended up as her lover, a third more valuable commodity would be required. She would have to like him. In the meantime, she gave all her attention to the city beyond the car window and immediately spotted a figure she knew.

Al Hutchinson was edging his way through the crowd which seemed to part like the Red Sea as he approached. No doubt they were as impressed as she was with the fact that he seemed at least eight inches taller than everyone else.

What sort of man was he, she wondered?

As she came to a conclusion, she let her eyes follow the broad shoulders of the square-jawed American as he dipped low and slipped into the biggest, shiniest car she had ever seen. Unlike the vehicles used by other passengers, it was neither a cab nor a chauffeur-driven limousine. Expensive as it no doubt was, there was a certain brashness about it, a lack of taste if not of wealth.

White tyres shone like tennis shoes against brown legs. The bodywork was dark yellow and the roof was black and looked to be fashioned from leather. Ideal, she thought, for the Italian climate. Ridiculous for England.

The thing that interested her most was that he had got in there alone. His blonde companion was nowhere in sight.

Virginia wondered where she was, and wondered what a New York gangster might be doing in the way of business in a town like Milan. The idea to follow him suddenly occurred to her. After all, he was now alone. Here was her chance. Perhaps she would bump into him at one of the museums or art galleries they were visiting.

As his car engine rumbled into life and drove away, she saw Zweizer and his sour-faced wife attempting to get into their hired vehicle. Elegant and well dressed as the woman was, no soft cut could relieve the angular shoulders, the shapeless hips. No make-up could give warmth to her face, nor add a smile to her mouth.

Zweizer tipped his hat in her direction and Virginia returned his smile.

'This is ours, Virginia,' she heard Raymonde say, and although she knew he had acquired a cab to take them on a sightseeing tour of the city, she could not help craning her neck, just like the jostling crowds.

'Virginia,' she heard him say again.

'Yes,' she said quickly before sliding into the back of the car. 'I'm sorry, Dorothy. I was just wondering who that little man was and why those people are watching him so intently.'

She did not see Raymonde's disbelieving glance.

Virginia then saw the person she was really seeking. Davis Sedglingham was standing quite still. Beneath a deep frown, his cool gaze stayed fixed on the small man who had made himself bigger by standing on a box. Whatever the man was saying had certainly taken Davis's fancy.

'The guy in the uniform said his name was Mussolini,' explained Raymonde. 'Ever heard of him?'

Virginia barely had time to shake her head before the cab was lurching forward and their English-speaking driver began to explain.

'He is Il Deuce!' he explained, his chest expanding like a fat pigeon and his face becoming pink with pride. 'He is the leader of the National Socialists. He will be a great man. Mark my words. The world will remember him.'

Virginia and Raymonde exchanged looks. They smiled at each other. The man was obviously biased. Not having noticed, nor caring about their reaction, he went on declaring his allegiance to the new party and its leader. Eventually, he got round to asking them exactly where they wanted to go.

'The Ambrosian Library,' Raymonde said quickly.

Virginia raised her eyebrows. 'That's news to me.'

Raymonde grinned and just remembered to keep his voice as feminine as possible.

'Trust me,' he murmured. He squeezed her hand.

In response, her eyes glittered like two diamonds. There was only the hint of a smile on her mouth, yet it was enough to make him wonder if she might care for him a bit more than she let on.

She did not speak for a while but just looked out of the cab window at the bustling crowds.

The voice of the cab driver filled most of the journey, his talk consisting of nothing but the rising power of the new order of things and his admiration for it.

Both Raymonde and Virginia remained silent. Raymonde wondered what Virginia might have in her mind. He would dearly love to be in there with her.

Virginia was wishing she could have followed Al Hutchinson. Something told her that her relationship with Davis Sedglingham was a non-starter. She had expected him to ask her to accompany him on his tour of Milan. To her dismay, he had not and she could not help wondering why. But she had no time to dwell on failure. There were other fish in the sea. The American seemed fair game and so did the Greek twins, although so far they had shown little interest.

Davis Sedglingham pushed his way through the crowds and into a small cafe where he could watch his fellow passengers get into the cabs provided by the company. Those that had paid the extra got into chauffeur-driven vehicles accompanied by at least one servant.

He sipped his coffee only once, then set it back down on the table. It was cold by the time he looked at his watch and made his way to the door.

Outside, even the crowd that had come to listen to the little man up on the box had started to filter away.

Davis took a deep breath, tugged at his brown tweed jacket until he was sure it hung neatly on his frame, then straightened his tie.

'Taxi!' He raised his ivory-topped cane as he shouted. A cab immediately came to a halt and he stepped in. 'One, one two, Via Sonora,' he said in English, then repeated it in Italian.

Petula Hutchinson, who was indeed Al's long suffering mate, if not his wife, watched with narrowed eyes as the honourable Englishman got himself into a cab and took off in a different direction to any of the other train passengers. Now why should that be, she asked herself? But she didn't dwell on it. Why should she? She was as glad to see the back of the rest of the passengers as she was of Al.

After buying some small trinket for her mother from a pretty little shop she found near the station, she made her way back onto the train.

Steam puffed around her ankles from the resting locomotive as she climbed back aboard.

'Let me help you, madam.' The voice was gentle. So was the kind hand that helped her.

Petula, who was more often called "honey" or "baby" by her current man, looked into the dark face of the man she knew to be the valet of the disdainful Englishman. She thanked him.

'Not with your boss then?' she asked once they were both aboard and heading towards their cabins.

'No, madam. I have things to do. Besides, Milan is not a place I like too much. I prefer Venice. I have relatives in Venice. But you, madam, why do you not enjoy the sights of this city?'

Petula came to a standstill outside her cabin door. Thoughtfully, she fiddled with her key. 'Al's got business. He's got business all over the place. I only came along for the ride, you could say.'

Mario nodded. 'I understand. But you do not wish to see the city.'

She shook her head. 'No. Not really. Seen one city, you've seen them all. I live in New York. I should know.

But deep at heart, I'm kind of a country girl myself. How about you?'

Mario's eyes brightened. It was the first time anyone on this journey had asked him his opinion. Even back in England, no one took much interest in what he thought or what he liked. He was just a valet and, at first of course, his English had not been too good, so they had avoided speaking to him anyway. Things were better now, but not much. Besides, his master barely gave him time to indulge in idleness.

'My father used to have a vineyard,' he explained. 'I like the country. I used to like to walk through the vines and smell the grapes growing.'

'Really? I didn't know you could smell grapes growing.'

The hard, defensive look that was usually on Petula's face, and which make-up failed to disguise, seemed to soften.

'Yes, yes.' Mario took a deep breath and closed his eyes as though he was back again in his father's vineyard and the smell of ripe grapes was heavy on the air. 'I can smell them even now.'

'Like corn, I suppose,' Petula added. She leaned her head on the honey-coloured wood of her cabin door. Her eyes took on a nostalgic look. 'I remember the smell of corn. I remember how blue the sky was too and how golden the corn looked against it. Like golden spears, I used to think. Golden spears, poking up to heaven.'

She laughed, and Mario, who had not laughed in a very long time, laughed with her.

It suddenly occurred to Petula just how good-looking the Italian was. True, he wasn't tall and he wasn't exactly slim. But he looked firm. The girth of his upper arms seemed to be fighting against the confines of his jacket and, although he was shorter than Al, his shoulders were just as broad and his waistline just as narrow.

There was something almost comical about his smile.

There was no surliness to it, no evidence that it could turn easily to a cruel sneer. He made her feel completely at ease and even affectionate.

'Come in and talk to me,' she said on a sudden impulse that might have been influenced by the throb of the bruises where Al's fingers had dug into her flesh.

Mario's eyes and mouth seemed to form a set of perfect ovals for a moment. Then he nodded, his face a picture of pleasure.

Petula rang for coffee and, while they waited, she asked Mario to tell her more about the vineyards and what he had done there.

He did exactly that. He spared no detail with regard to either his desire or the description of the body of the girl he had lusted for the most.

By the time the coffee arrived, Petula was breathing a little more heavily than she had been. She took a quick sip of coffee followed by another – as if that might take her mind off the fact that her camisole seemed suddenly to be made of sacking rather than silk because her nipples were hardening and expanding even though they had no room in which to do so. They pulsed almost painfully as they engorged with blood and desire. Between her thighs, she felt a slow, creeping sensation. It was as though her pubic hair had become electrified and was moving around like a nest of ardent vipers.

At last she found her voice. 'That was a very,' she paused as she fought over which word to use, 'arousing story.'

Mario, his dark face wrinkled with smiles and his eyes hardly leaving her face, merely nodded.

Petula took a deep breath. 'I suppose I could tell you more about the cornfield.' She sighed, then raised her hand to her mouth. Old thoughts and old romances came to her mind. Thinking of them added deeper colour to her rouged cheeks. 'That cornfield could certainly tell some tales,' she added.

Mario rested his elbows on his knees, hands clasped in front of him. Without saying a word, he eyed her expectantly.

Petula took a deep breath. Generalisations about the cornfield were over. Now she had to dredge her mind for the more explicit, more lurid details.

'Harvesting was the best,' she began. 'You know, the prairies stretch every way as far as the eye can see. And the corn was taller than I was.

'My, but I'd get so hot helping with that harvest. All I wanted to do was strip off and run naked through the stalks of corn. One day, when I was hot as a Thanksgiving turkey just out from the oven, I did exactly that.

'I found a clump of corn away from where everyone else was sat eating their lunch. I took off everything. It was great. The breeze coming over the prairie cooled me. I lifted my arms above my head, bent my head backwards and closed my eyes. The sun still kissed my face, but the shadows from the standing corn and the breeze cooled my body. If I thought about it really hard, I could imagine the breeze was someone's hands; long, cool, soft hands – light as cobwebs as they ran over my body. Then suddenly they were hands, only this time they belonged to Jeb, a guy who helped on the farm at times.'

Petula paused for effect, but also because her mouth was dry and her own story was causing her body to get just as hot as it had on the prairie that day.

Mario was staring at her. His jaw hung slack and his eyes were wide.

'Go on,' he urged, his voice husky with feeling. 'Go on. Tell me what happened. Tell me what you did together.'

Petula glanced to a point between Mario's open knees. She knew a large erection when she saw one and, as she continued her story, her gaze left his crotch only to glance up into his eyes. It was just to confirm that her story was having the right effect.

'Jeb was a good-looking guy. He had a good body, and I knew he had one helluva prick. I'd seen plenty enough of him when he and the other guys were diving into the creek. They never wore swimsuits.

'All the same, I only gave him one glance. I still had this weird notion that it was really the breeze making love to me. Somehow, it was more thrilling to think that. More arousing. Jeb knocked some of the cobs to the ground and wound some of the corn fronds around my wrists way above my head. I didn't protest. It was a lovely feeling to be stretched out like that whilst he made love to me. It was like being worshipped – you know, like being some stretched-out goddess or something. I could have got myself loose of course, but I didn't want to. I just wanted him to do everything. It was too hot for me to want to wrap my arms around him, so I didn't.'

Once she had stopped speaking, she looked directly into Mario's eyes. He said nothing to her. Neither of them needed to add anything to the story she had just told. It was as if each one was reaching into the other's mind, searching for the right words that would take them out of storytelling and into actuality.

Mario got there first. He licked his lips and cleared his throat before he spoke.

'I should think that would be a very nice thing – to have you wrap your arms around me. I should think it would be very nice indeed.'

Petula stared at him. Things were happening to her that prevented her from speaking. What were those things, she asked herself? She tried to concentrate, to turn her mind inwards so she could understand better.

Were her breasts about to burst through her camisole, or was she merely imagining it? Were her pubic hairs dancing over her skin, her sex seeping with desire?

She made a decision, then slowly rose to her feet, walked over to Mario and took his face in her hands.

'I should think it would be very nice if I put my arms around you,' she said. 'I think it would be nice for me as well as you.'

Mario, eyes blazing with passion, also got to his feet.

There were no more words as they wrapped their arms around each other, holding one another very tightly.

No more than an inch remained between their lips as they looked into each other's eyes. Both had an instinctive knowledge that they had more than one thing in common. Both knew that nothing was going to stop what was about to happen.

Even as their lips met, their embrace tightened. An urgency swept over them as though they had not tasted the likes of each other ever before.

'There's satin sheets on my bed,' Petula whispered breathlessly when she had at last extricated her mouth from his. 'They sure would feel cool against our bodies. Just like that breeze did in that old cornfield. What do you say?'

Clothes were left on the floor. Not that it mattered whether the sheets were satin or cotton, cool or hot. The heat of their bodies warmed the slippery fabric.

Petula groaned with delight as she felt the wiry hair of Mario's chest against her breasts. Her nipples, which had thrust so demandingly against her camisole, now nuzzled in the thick mat of fur.

They lay on their sides and, as Mario's prick divided one sexual flap from another, Petula lifted one leg and draped it across his.

Their kisses were full of passion, yet there was no bruising in them, only a mutual pleasure, a new and delightful affection.

Mario's fingers did not dig into Petula's flesh like Al's had done. On the contrary, his palms caressed her from shoulder to thigh. His fingers drew soothing circles down her back, her arms and her buttocks. As his fingers cares-

sed, the discomfort left behind by Al's abuse of her seemed
to melt away.

Normally, she might have used her nails to rake his back,
to rake that of any man who took her. But she did not do
this to Mario.

Instead, she caressed his cheeks, her fingers following the
line of his brow, the hollows beneath his cheekbones, the
sensual smile of his mouth.

In time her hand ran down over his belly, her fingers
dividing when she met his cock which was already inside
her, already slippery with her juices.

Chapter 12

Any city under the sun caters for all the sins that are known to man, and Milan, Davis Sedglingham knew, was no exception.

'I want you to take me to the best house in the city,' he said to the taxi driver.

The driver had given him a furtive look as he swiftly transferred the two hundred lire note from his fare's hand and into his pocket.

He did not question Davis as to what address this house might have. He knew too well that the word "house" had been applied in a very liberal way indeed. This man wanted a house where women truly "worked" for their living.

They left the wide esplanades and baroque grandeur of a city built by the wealthy for the wealthy. The roads they traversed became narrower and the houses they passed were not of the same splendid design as those in the heart of the city. Nevertheless, they had been grand once and still were, though their style was not currently in favour.

'Wait for me,' Davis ordered the driver when at last they came to a halt.

The driver merely nodded, tipped his cap over his eyes, and sank back into his seat.

What did he care about waiting around whilst this Englishman paid some whore for instant relief. After all, what could be better than being paid to do nothing?

Davis paused at the foot of some steps that led up to the building. Of course he could have spent some more time with the beautiful Virginia but, alluring as she was, she lacked the one attribute that might have made him ask her to marry him. She had no wealth. At least, not according to that clumsy-looking woman who travelled with her. He understood that she wasn't exactly poor, but she had no inheritance to come from rich relatives. Rich relatives were definitely a prerequisite to being wealthy for life. It was a shame his own dear father had let it slide so easily through his fingers. It was also a shame that he had passed on those same lackadaisical characteristics to his son.

No, thought Davis. This house and the women within it would give him what he wanted until he allowed himself to be seen in public with someone who could save his ailing fortunes.

Whistling blithely and twirling the ebony cane he carried, he started up the steps.

The house had a row of pillars along its front, the sort more suited to a temple than a house. A house of love, Davis mused.

On the first floor, narrow windows looked out from above an intricate pattern of multicoloured tiling. The windows were arched in the Norman manner, a style in fashion when de Vinci painted, just before Columbus discovered the New World.

Davis strode up the steps in the manner of a man who knew what he wanted and was used to getting it. Taking hold of his cane halfway down its length, he rapped three times on the stout, studded door. That was before he saw the wrought-iron bell pull. He gave it a hefty tug and heard its note resound somewhere deep inside.

The door opened and, instead of coming face to face with some hard-eyed madam or some courteous servant, he saw nothing but empty air.

'Seigneur. Monsieur. Sir?' Three languages for the same word.

He looked down. Large blue eyes in a large head, which

in turn sat atop a squat body, looked up at him.

'I was recommended,' he said with a lofty air.

'Sir,' said the dwarf, opening the door wider so that this new customer could enter.

Once inside, Davis was instantly convinced he had come to a classy establishment. Not for this place the cheap red plush upholstery that some establishments in London seemed to think was suited to its profession.

This place was the epitome of Italian understatement. Murals depicting hunting scenes, satyrs ravishing wood nymphs and curving mermaids obliging grateful sailors with their mouths covered the walls.

Furniture that owed more to the court of Louis XIV than to a bawdy house was set discreetly behind groups of jardinières, silk screens, and painted pillars.

There was no sign of any women and, just for a moment, Davis wondered whether he had come to the right place. He decided that he had. After all, the driver was waiting for him outside.

The dwarf waddled to a small table, picked up a glass bell and rang it. Then he bowed and, with a bustling, incredibly quick gait, he was gone.

A draft of air wafted around Davis's calves as a door opened in the far corner of the room.

Davis turned to face it. Again, this madam was nothing like the sort he was used to in London.

Silently, the woman glided towards him.

He could see she was studying him, her eyes taking in every detail.

At the same time, he let his gaze wander from her neatly shingled black hair which clung so tightly around her heart-shaped face, over the neat black suit she was wearing, all the way down to her feet.

What surprised him most about her was the fact that she was wearing a man's suit, a waistcoat, even a tie. Her eyes were outlined with blackness. Her lips were bright red.

'What might I do for you, sir?'

She spoke in clear, precise English. It surprised him that she had categorised him correctly, until he realised that she had studied his clothes more so than his body. Experience had obviously taught her something about clothes and their origins. Savile Row was recognisable the world over. Full of his own self-confidence and painfully aware that his member was already demanding to be satisfied, he pulled off his gloves. Both them, the hat and the cane were taken from him by the self-same dwarf who had opened the front door.

'A girl, please madam. Your best girl.' He repeated his statement because he wanted no cheating from this woman. He knew what madams were like the world over. Money from his wallet had found many a home in their hot, grasping little hands. But oh, what delights he got in return!

The woman, who he judged to be about forty years of age but still worth more than a second glance, did not smile. She merely nodded in a very perfunctory manner and eyed him again.

'And my best price, sir? Are you willing to pay me generously for supplying this girl?'

Davis reached for his wallet. 'Whatever you want,' he said as he started to undo it. He halted. 'But no cheating, mind you. I'll not pay for a girl who doesn't please me.'

The madam, her eyes firmly fixed on Davis's wallet, nodded again. 'I understand, sir. Only the best. And you have come to the right place, sir, because here, at Castell Monte Veneto, we only have the very best.'

Chapter 13

Agnetha Zweizer bid her husband a hasty, if not a frosty goodbye. He had expressed his intention to visit an old banking acquaintance whilst he was in Milan.

'If you must, then you must,' she exclaimed, sighing as the driver came to a stop near the imposing facade of a building that must only have been built during the last few years, judging by its austere lines. Iron bars separated the glass of the windows from the world outside. There was no doubting that the building was a bank even without reading the gold letters embossed in bluish-grey granite by the entrance.

'Do enjoy your shopping, my dear,' said her husband before the car door closed and the chauffeur took her away.

Zweizer slowly ascended the steps, his eyes glancing furtively at the car until it had become at one with the busy city.

Without even getting to the door, he turned quickly round, his breathing becoming as animated as his steps. He peered down the road to see the car turn a corner and finally disappear. He stopped at the edge of the pavement, looked in the other direction and raised his walking stick. A taxi cab saw him and skidded to a halt, dust rising from the road and coating the spokes of the wheels.

Without a backward glance at the bank, Zweizer gave the driver directions and slid into the back seat.

Banks, offices and municipal establishments gave way to avenues and piazzas where buildings founded in another age stood shoulder to shoulder.

Zweizer sighed with happiness, his bulk half filling the space in the back seat.

At last the taxi came to a halt in front of an imposing place that Zweizer barely glanced at. If he had, he would have noted, as Davis Sedglingham had done, that it dated from the Middle Ages. Because of his banking interests, Zweizer was a man who had travelled, and Milan was one of those places he had visited before.

There was another taxi in front of them and Zweizer gave that little regard either. The driver appeared to be snoozing, his cap tilted forward over his face.

'Wait for me,' said Zweizer to the cab driver, his voice breathless with excitement.

With glazed eyes, his tongue continuously sweeping over his bottom lip, Zweizer puffed and panted his way to the front door. He ignored the wrought-iron bell pull and immediately heaved on the heavy knocker.

As the echoes of his insistent knocking fell away, the door opened.

The dwarf immediately recognised him and Zweizer stepped inside.

The dwarf spoke to him in French and Zweizer replied in the same language.

'Madame will be with you shortly.'

'It will be delightful to meet her again.' He quickly handed his hat, coat and walking stick over to the small man. Even before the dwarf had disappeared with the bundle that seemed larger than he did, the same tall woman who had greeted Davis Sedglingham, now welcomed Henrich Zweizer to her select establishment.

'And what is your delight for today, Herr Zweizer? Your usual?'

Zweizer nodded, his dancing eyes and open jaw betraying his great need.

'Then come this way,' said the unsmiling madam, and Zweizer went, automatically knowing that they were to

110

mount the wide staircase and follow the sweeping balustrade that would bring them onto a broad balcony that overlooked the room below.

Footsteps barely audible, their sound muffled in the thickness of the carpet, man followed woman until they stopped before a door on which the madam knocked. Without waiting for an answer, she entered.

Zweizer's hand went to his throat which suddenly felt very tight. His gaze was firmly fixed to where the delectable creature with blue eyes and very dark hair lay on the bed. She was wearing the flimsiest of peignoirs and the silkiest of stockings held up by garters that seemed no more than blue ribbons.

'May I have the lights turned down?' asked Zweizer haltingly.

'Certainly, monsieur,' the madam replied.

Her adjustment of the gas lights, which were wall mounted and covered with crystal shades, was quickly undertaken.

'You prefer me in this half-light?' asked the young woman on the bed, her expression questioning and without the trace of a smile.

'Yes,' replied Zweizer. 'I like you in this light very much indeed. You remind me of someone. Someone who has had quite an effect on me.'

Zweizer hardly noticed the door closing behind him. His hands were already on his clothes, fingers fumbling and falling over each other as his ardour and his speed increased.

'Do you want me to call for a valet?' asked the young woman.

Zweizer shook his head so frantically that his jowls wobbled like jelly against his collar.

'No. I can manage. Damn!' he added as a button flew across the room.

'I'll ring,' declared the young woman, her face as inscrutable as before.

111

Such was his ardour that Zweizer didn't really care that the valet who came and assisted him saw his fat body without clothes and without dignity.

He didn't even care that the man stayed to fold and hang up his clothes as he himself clambered onto the bed beside the young woman.

However, he did nothing too exuberant until the valet had left the room with Zweizer's shoes, declaring that he would put them outside the door after he had given them a good buffing.

Zweizer wanted to answer that he would do the same – to this young woman. But he was beyond quick ripostes. His erection was big in size and in appetite, and this girl was willing. That she was being paid for her services was neither here nor there.

'Virginia,' Zweizer murmured as he kissed the girl's face.

'My name is Lola,' she explained. 'As you already know. But if you want to call me Virginia, I am quite happy for you to do that.'

Chapter 14

Agnetha Zweizer snuggled down into the fur collar of her Astrakhan coat and smiled secretively to herself.

The hard lines of her face seemed to melt and her eyes, which sometimes seemed to be mere chips of coal in her eye sockets, became warmer, their colour changing to resemble old brandy. Like a tight bud touched by spring sunshine, she suddenly seemed to flower.

She stretched her neck away from her collar and smoothed her hair away from her face. Being a lady of some advancing years, she was glad her hair was fair and thus any grey was easily comouflaged.

She reached forward, lay her hand on the shoulder of her driver and rubbed it affectionately. Her voice was like honey.

'Hans, my darling. How did you manage it?'

Because he was driving, the blond Adonis she addressed could only give her a cursory glance, but she saw his smile.

She caught her breath as his hand covered hers.

'For you, my darling Agnetha, my lady of the bed chamber, I can move mountains.'

Agnetha purred like a kitten, though in actual fact she was way past being even a young pussy. 'Hans, you never cease to amaze me. Did you do some shopping for me?'

He laughed. 'Of course. A few select items – a bracelet, earrings. Small enough in size, but big enough in outlay. Your husband will be convinced that you have indeed been shopping. I used the money you gave me.'

'What a man you are, and what a lucky lady I am to be loved by someone like you. What would I do without you my gorgeous, beautiful man?'

Hans chuckled again. 'Never mind what you would do without me. Today you will show me what you can do when you are with me. I have booked us a room at the Milan Astoria. The oysters sit there in their shiny little shells and the champagne is getting colder and colder in its bucket of ice. The sheets on the bed are pulled back. Everything is ready for us.'

'Darling,' cried Agnetha, and could not resist planting a deep and succulent kiss on the nape of his neck. 'You think of everything.' And her voice trembled with expectation.

'No,' he said. 'I think of one thing only. That is the trouble. I only think of you. Especially at night when you are lying untouched beside that fat pig of a husband of yours. As he snores beside you, I lie in my bed and play with myself. I make believe it is you who pulls on me. I make believe it is your body my seed spills over and not just a cotton sheet.'

Chapter 15

'Would you really become Sedglingham's mistress?'

Raymonde tottered as he asked Virginia the question. He was unaccustomed to wearing women's shoes and, once they reached Istanbul, he had no intention of ever wearing them again.

'If he asks me,' she responded. She paused before shooting him a slight smile over her shoulder. 'Are you jealous?'

She turned swiftly away again before he had a chance to answer, her heels tapping a quick step on the museum's marble floor as they exited the building. A flight of wide steps lay before them.

'No. Just concerned.'

'Why?'

As they reached the bottom of the steps, Raymonde reached for her arm so she had to stop and wait for him.

'Virginia, please don't try to fool me. I saw the look on your face last night after he left. You've got second thoughts about him.'

Virginia's smile disappeared. She glared as she looked directly into Raymonde's face, the man who at present knew her body more intimately than anyone.

'It's none of your business!' she snapped. 'You're only the hired help. Remember?'

She shrugged his hand off as she looked at her wristwatch. It had been made by Cartier and bought for her by her previous lover. Looking at it gave her an instant reminder of the first time she had seen it. He had lain it across her naked belly. She remembered it feeling cold against her flesh – just as at the moment the silk lining of her coat was cool against her hidden nakedness. But the closeness of her lover's body had never affected her in the same way that Raymonde did. She made a bid to regain her self-control.

'Stop interrogating me. We have to get back or the train will be leaving without us.'

'What's the rush? Congested as this town is, the taxi only takes half an hour.'

Virginia hunched her shoulders and sighed impatiently. Raymonde, she decided, was taking too much upon himself. She began to stride away from him. Her voice rang in his ears. 'We're not going by taxi. We're walking.'

Raymonde stared after her, attempted a few steps, tottered and came to a halt.

His face became contorted as he bent down and took off the offending shoes.

'Damn!' he shouted after her. 'Well, I'm not walking. I'm getting a taxi and that's that!'

Virginia took no notice.

Raymonde picked up the shoes, swore again, then waved one at a taxi. When he next looked to where she had stalked off, Virginia was nowhere in sight.

Virginia herself did not stop to see if Raymonde was following her. Such was her faith in his adoration and her own powers of control, she was sure that he must be.

It wasn't until she had turned down the narrower streets, and from them down narrower alleys, that she realised she was completely alone. Even so, she would not allow panic to set in. Not yet. Still, she trembled beneath the coat that covered her nakedness and her face became flushed with sudden anxiety.

Lines of washing flapped from seedy tenements and round-eyed children with hungry expressions and shabby clothes sat in the street and watched her pass. Their mothers eyed her suspiciously from the safety of their own doorways, their dark eyes wary with envy and suspicion.

Only the fact that she had been born into poverty prevented Virginia from panicking. How well she remembered streets like these in London's East End. How well she remembered making a special effort to learn how to speak well, how to dress well and, best of all, how to make love well.

She made a great effort to smile at the children and nod at the mothers as she passed by.

'Keep your head,' she told herself. But she knew animosity when she saw it. She also knew that not only poor people lived in such places. So did the criminal, the wretched and the mad. As she thought those thoughts, her step quickened.

Panic would not be denied. No longer did she carefully pick her way through the filthy puddles. Fear overcame fastidiousness. Three alleys led off from the one she was in. Which one? She chose that which had the least shadows and the least number of people leaning in darkened doorways.

Relief came once she found the alley she was walking along opening up into a small, shabby piazza. She took a deep breath as she swiftly came into sunlight, walked a few steps forward, then stopped to catch her breath.

She had seen far more stylish places, but at this moment in time this was the most beautiful piazza she had ever laid eyes on.

No marble slabs and pruned trees decorated this particular square, although it did have a fountain in the middle of it.

At the sight of the tumbling water, Virginia rushed forward and scooped palmfuls of it into her hands and over her face. It felt so hot, as did the body beneath the coat. If she had been wearing a dress she would have taken her coat off. She cursed her foolishness. Why hadn't she just

117

stuck to wearing no knickers? That in itself would have been exciting enough.

Only when she straightened was she fully aware of just how silent the square was. From what she had been told both by fellow travellers and the official brochure, it seemed totally out of character for Italy. Where were the usual groups of men playing chequers and suchlike?

The square was completely empty and silent except for the cooing of nearby doves and the scratching of a mangy dog who lay dozing in the sun.

More concerned than her expression gave away, Virginia looked back at the alley she had come through and wondered whether she could find her way back along it to where she had left Raymonde.

Silently, she cursed him. Why hadn't he followed her? She ignored the fact that it was her own foolish pride, her conceit that he was her slave and would do anything for her.

Her eyes searched the square, centred on the other alleys that ran between sleepy houses where yellow, green and brown stucco peeled off in blistering patches.

Which way, she asked herself? Which way?

A sharp, loud crack suddenly sounded. Pigeons, disturbed from their midday snooze, shot up into the air, a mass of feathers and fluttering wings.

Panic was overcome but Virginia felt confused. Did she recognise that sound? She had a feeling she did.

Suddenly, before the pigeons barely had time to resettle in their favourite roosts, a second crack sounded.

'My God!' exclaimed Virginia. 'It's a gun.'

She stared in the direction from where she thought the shot had come. Self-preservation overcame curiosity.

Wary and now fully alert to the fact that she was in a foreign country that had experienced some political upheavals of late, she ran across to the north side of the square and backed into a doorway that was half hidden by shadows.

It was not a moment too soon. Running footsteps in one of the adjacent alleys became louder. They were coming her way. She pressed herself more tightly against the door behind her.

There was darkness all around. Sunlight bathed the square before her eyes. Then suddenly, it was blanked out from her vision.

A man with wild eyes appeared in front of her. He looked surprised to see her there. She started, wanted to scream. Fear replaced surprise on the young man's face.

From where she stood, Virginia smelt his body and his fear. His hair and face were wet with sweat and blood.

She cried a small cry and raised her hand before her face. The smell of sweat still assaulted her senses.

He seemed to hang there, his hands bracing him in the stone surround of the doorway. Like his face, his hands were also wet with sweat and blood. She noticed something else too.

She looked again and stared at the gun that hung from his left hand.

A gun! He was going to kill her.

'Oh no,' she muttered. 'Don't kill me. Not now. Not dressed like this.'

He cocked his head and frowned. 'English?'

The young man was speaking to her, yet what he said seemed to take a long time to sink into her brain.

'English?' he repeated again. His bruised jaw hung open. His breath came in short, sharp gasps as though his chest were hurting him.

'Yes.' She nodded. Stupid to think amusing thoughts at such a time, but she wondered whether he was out hunting for tourists! 'Don't be an idiot,' she warned herself.

With obvious agitation, the young man looked behind him towards the direction he had come

He looked back at her and, as he did so, a lopsided grin appeared. He winced. Obviously grinning hurt him. She wondered how many of his teeth were broken and, as she wondered, a mix of saliva and blood ran from the corner of his mouth.

'Do not be afraid. I am not going to hurt you.' His voice was coarse, though surprisingly gentle.

Virginia took a thankful breath. 'Good. I'm glad about that.'

A puzzled frown appeared again on his face. He cocked his head to one side.

'I do not think I will shoot you. You are too pretty a woman for me to want to kill you. But if you are rich then I will take you with me.' He made a grab for her arm. 'How much ransom would I get for you?'

He tried to drag her from the doorway. She braced her legs, refused to move. She had to gain time for his pursuers to catch up with him.

It was a wild thought and a wild gesture, but to Virginia it seemed her only hope.

With a swiftness born of self-preservation, she undid the buttons of her coat and swept it away from her body.

The young man gasped. His eyes stared and all the fear in them was suddenly replaced with sheer lust.

'*Mama mia!*'

Still with the gun in his hand, he reached out. As he trailed his fingers over her naked flesh, she felt also the touch of the cold steel weapon. She shivered.

Her breasts rose and fell more quickly. Her breathing began to match his as both his hand and the gun were pressed against her breast.

'Have you any money?' he suddenly asked.

She sighed, disappointed that he really was no more than a mere robber. But perhaps he was also a liar and might shoot her yet. Handsome as he was, she couldn't help welcoming the sound of more running footsteps. They were accompanied by a male voice shouting, orders being barked out in quick succession.

Police, she thought, or military.

She saw the fear in his eyes.

As he tugged her handbag from her grasp, he kissed her cheek.

'I'll get your bag back to you,' he cried, then was gone.

Virginia wrapped her coat back around her. There was barely time to rebutton it before the silent square was a mass of moving men and shouting people.

Those living behind the crumbling edifices that surrounded the square now woke from their slumbers and reveries to throw open blinds and shout opinions of what was going on to their neighbours.

Before she had time to make herself completely presentable, three soldiers were standing before her, their bayonets pointing in her direction.

One of them barked an order.

Virginia took a deep breath and raised her head high. 'I'm sorry,' she exclaimed in a high and mighty fashion. 'I'm English. I don't understand what you're saying.'

'You sound like a memsahib,' she told herself. Never mind. At times like these it paid to be overbearing. Anything was better than showing fear.

One of the soldiers shouted something over his shoulder.

Like the parting of the Red Sea, the whole bunch of them edged aside as another man with a more flamboyant uniform and feathers in his hat filled her eyes and blocked the view of the square.

Virginia shrank back.

She didn't like the hardness in this man's eyes, the squareness of his unrelenting features, the thin mouth, the black moustache.

A gold filling glinted as he smiled. His eyes swept her body, the clenched fists and the coat she gripped in her hands. She immediately read all the signs of what he intended to do. He turned to his men and ordered them away.

Virginia shivered. There was only him between her and

121

freedom. Dare she make an attempt to escape?

She assessed her chances. Granted she might be able to aim a kick at his crotch and duck under his arm. But what about when she got into the square? One word of command to his soldiers and she could be lying dead.

The officer turned back to her. He seemed familiar, though she couldn't say why.

In a sudden show of courtesy, he took off his hat and bowed in an abrupt manner.

'Lieutenant Andreas Corellia, Miss Vernon. At your service.' Once his hat was back on his head, he saluted her.

Virginia looked at him in surprise.

'How did you know . . .?'

'I saw you at the station, Miss Vernon. Perhaps you could tell me why you are so far from your train.'

Virginia heaved a sigh of relief before speaking. 'You know me?' she asked querulously.

He came a little closer. His gold filling seemed to be reflected by a glint in his eyes.

'You would not have noticed, Miss Vernon. You swept past me with barely a glance in my direction. But I spoke to the lady who was with you. I like to find out about people that interest me. Finding you here at the same time as an escaped felon is of even more interest to me. Now. Tell me what you know about Alphonse Ameretti.'

Virginia looked bemused. 'If you mean the man who just ran off with my handbag, I know nothing at all about him.'

She winced as the back of the officer's hand landed with enough force on her cheek to jerk her head to one side.

'You had better be telling the truth, Miss Vernon.'

Whilst rubbing her scalding cheek, she blinked and concentrated her gaze on the officer.

'I *am* telling the truth. I got lost. The man you want demanded money, then he heard you coming so he snatched my handbag and ran away.'

The officer raised his hand again.

'It's the truth,' Virginia blurted, and before she remembered that her coat was still half undone, she had raised her hands before her face.

A pale pink nipple broke through the opening. Its appearance did not go unnoticed.

Virginia sucked in her breath and tried not to show the fear she was feeling inside.

The officer was no longer looking at her face. His eyes were on her naked breast. His hand slid beneath her coat and covered it.

'*Bellissima*!' the officer exclaimed, his eyes bright, his tongue slippery and wet as it slid over his lips.

She shivered at his touch, but instinctively knew she must not show any repugnance. She must submit.

As he squeezed her breast, she wondered if this same hand had also been responsible for the blood that ran over Alphonse Ameretti's face and hands. Somewhere, she guessed, there was a place where the police and military committed acts of torture. That was where the fugitive must have escaped from. It was a place that she must seek to avoid.

Her thoughts gave wings to her fear. She could not allow either morals or shyness to impair her chance of escape.

Slowly, as the officer concentrated on squeezing her bosom, she undid those buttons she had managed to do up.

Suddenly her coat was open.

She took hold of its front edges and spread them wide.

All the officer's hardness lessened – at least it did on his face and in his frame.

Virginia noticed movement in his loins. But then, how could he not become erect at the sight of her?

There she was, coat spread wide, clad only in a white turban, matching shoes and silk stockings held up with a pair of pretty garters.

'Do you believe me now, lieutenant?' she purred. 'As you can see, I have nothing to hide.' She opened her legs slightly. His eyes went to the patch of glossy hair that nestled like silk between her legs. She saw him sniff, knew he was smelling her sex.

She could see he was wondering what to do next. Was she to go to some hidden torture chamber, or was he to settle the matter here and now?

He made a low, murmuring kind of sound before he answered. 'I will tell you in a moment when I have finished with you.'

She had won, though he could not possibly know that.

Before her eyes, he quickly loosened his belt then undid the buttons of his flies.

Her eyes followed the progress of his hand as he pulled his member away from his body and out into the air.

He looked at her proudly and waved his weapon as though he were going to beat her with it. It was certainly big enough.

Virginia took a deep breath. Could she manage such a large penis? It was no less than ten inches long and of a generous circumference.

She looked up into his face, saw the cruelty behind the lust, and decided she had no choice.

He entered her first from the front, his hands playing with her breasts as he thrust into her.

She groaned and at one stage she couldn't help but cry out. He was such a well-endowed man, too big even for someone of her experience. Her cries would have got much louder if he hadn't muffled them with his hand. He covered her mouth until every last inch of him was tightly embedded in her vagina.

'My legs will snap,' she thought to herself as the muscles of her inner thighs stretched as her legs opened.

At last the rough crispness of his pubic hair was mingling with hers. His uniform rubbed against her bare flesh whilst his hands rubbed her breasts and his fingers pulled and pinched at her nipples.

Virginia was aware that a line of soldiers stood between the officer's back and the square. There was a low hum of voices now. Some of the braver souls in the neighbourhood were out in the square, discussing what might be taking place but not daring to question.

The roofs of the buildings and the strip of blue sky she could see over the officer's shoulder seemed to dance and gyrate as the big man slammed himself into her.

He grunted against her ear, his hands beneath her coat, clutching her buttocks and steadying her each time he pulled out then rammed himself back into her.

Despite the danger of her predicament and the fact that this man had given her no choice about having sex with him, Virginia could not help but respond.

It was as though her senses had taken over, allied, she thought, to her need for self-preservation. No doubt the fact that his penis was too big to ignore helped intensify the pleasure she was feeling.

Sensations that started as mere pinpricks of delight came into existence. The pinpricks intensified, became more liquid, more electric as they spread over and within her flesh.

She began to moan as pleasure overcame fear, her hips meeting his thrusts as though urging him to greater things.

Instinctively, she knew there was a need for urgency. This man had no intention of controlling his release until she reached an orgasm. His only aim was that he reached his as quickly as possible.

But Virginia would not allow him to use her purely for his own pleasure. She had every intention of eliciting her own climax from this liaison.

Suddenly, she opened her eyes wide and her thrusts towards him became more vigorous. Each time she jerked her hips to meet his, she made the same groaning noise he did.

Responding to this sudden enthusiasm with surprise written all over his face, the officer looked down at her. His mouth was now hanging open, his breath coming in quick, sharp gasps in tune with his hips.

His eyes were wide. Virginia could almost read his mind. He might retreat from her. After all, he was a man who had tortured another man. Wouldn't that be the ultimate torture if he pulled himself out from her and left her with no climax?

But, of course, he couldn't do that. His own climax was well on its way, his semen already coursing up through his stem.

Virginia could feel his penis pulsing inside her, phallic palpitations throbbing against her muscles.

Like a cool, rushing wave, her climax finally hit her, lifting her up on its crest, dancing around her like a cloud of spray, until it fell away, fading to nothing except a flurry of ebbing ripples.

As if she had given him a cue, the officer tensed against her. His arms clasped her tightly to him as he throbbed into her, his stiff flesh filling her with its hardness and its seed until there was no more to give and no hardness remaining.

As the weight of his arms left her, Virginia straightened, took a deep breath and patted her hair.

The officer stared at her, then roughly reached for her coat which still hung open.

'Have you no shame, woman?' he growled as he re-buttoned it.

Virginia regarded him with abject coolness, her chin high, her eyes blazing.

'Have you, lieutenant? You were the one who took advantage of a woman alone. The shame is yours, lieutenant, not mine.'

There was confusion in his eyes, a trembling around his lips. 'I believe you enjoyed what I did to you.'

She looked at him with more defiance. 'You took advantage of my body, lieutenant. It seemed only fair that I take advantage of yours.'

He remained speechless as she brushed past him and swept out into the square.

Curious faces of townspeople and soldiers eyed her as she stood there, arms wrapped around herself, looking back to where the officer was straightening his uniform as he stepped out into the sunlight.

'I must get back to the station,' she said, her voice authoritative at the same time as being alluringly seductive. 'I must depend on you to get me there. After all, I have no handbag now. No money to pay for a taxi.'

He took a deep breath before he clicked his heels and saluted her.

'This way, signora.' He pointed her in the direction of a black-painted staff car.

Perfectly controlled despite her ordeal, Virginia walked towards it, then waited by the door until he had opened it and helped her in.

When she got back to the station Raymonde, looking the epitome of a distraught and spinsterish travelling companion, was pacing up and down, eyes scanning the crowded station. The moment he spotted her with the officer he had seen earlier, he knew what had happened.

There was a dancing excitement in her eyes and an oddly furtive though triumphant look in that of the officer.

Raymonde waited for Virginia to bid the man adieu. He had no wish to make the acquaintance of the officer again, though Virginia could not possibly guess as to why.

Virginia left the lieutenant with a slightly offended look on his face.

'What did you say to him?' Raymonde asked her. 'He didn't look too happy.'

Virginia smiled sideways at him. She was like a cat, he thought, when she did that. A sleek, sensual feline who

127

would stretch, purr and undulate when caressed by an affectionate hand.

She chuckled to herself and at first he thought she was not going to tell him. Was it jealousy that made him exclaim?

'Well?'

'Sorry to be late, Dorothy darling,' said Virginia lightly, winking as she smiled up at Raymonde. 'Aren't you going to ask me where I've been and what I've been doing?'

Her toying with him changed his mood. He sighed as he helped her onto the train.

'No,' he muttered through half-closed lips. 'I only wanted to know what you said to the guy with the shiny buttons and the shooter on his hip. I already know more or less what's been going on.'

Virginia looked at him with surprise. He leaned closer to her ear. 'We have an extra passenger on board. He's brought your bag with him and he reckons on coming across the border with us.'

Virginia was about to walk down the corridor that led to the privacy of her cabin and her washroom. Raymonde's remark, more so than his hand on her bottom, made her stop in her tracks.

'What? He's here? That young man's here?'

'Shhh!' Raymonde put a finger to his lips. 'Not so loud.'

Virginia frowned. 'What do you mean – not so loud! Why haven't you turned him over to the guard?'

Raymonde tilted his head to one side. 'Why did you look at that officer guy as though he was something stuck on your shoe?'

Virginia lowered her eyes. 'If he hadn't been wearing that uniform, I might have acted differently. I wonder if uniforms change people for the worse?'

'If you listen to the guy that's sitting on your bed, you'll get confirmation. He's adamant that come hell or high water, he's crossing the border with us.'

128

'He's got to be joking. He'll get us all shot!'

'From what he's already told me, if he's found in your cabin we'll all be shot anyway!'

Chapter 16

Sensibly, Raymonde had drawn the curtains. The warm luxury of the very best accommodation on the train was lit by a single wall light. So subtle was its glow, that only one half of their features were highlighted. One cheekbone, one side of each jaw was bathed in a soft amber light and eyes seemed dark and unfathomable in their sockets.

A sudden sparkle in the darkness of Alphonse Ameretti's eyes immediately took Virginia back to that brief moment in a shaded doorway when he had paused to ogle her naked body, even though a whole battalion of soldiers were pursuing him. Such a thought made her shiver with satisfaction.

The vision immediately disappeared as he sprang to his feet, his expression one of fear and pleading.

'Signora, I am so sorry I have to take advantage of you like this. I do apologise. Believe me, I would not have done so if I had not been in danger of my life!'

There was no saluting or clicking of heels with this man. Granted, his face bore the signs of violence, an open cut above one eye from which the crusted blood had been cleaned away. Yet, despite the strength of his features and the firm set of his jaw, there was pleading in his eyes and also gentleness.

I think I can understand that.' Virginia's voice was steady though she could barely keep her eyes off him. All the same, it was hard to believe this was happening.

He came closer.

'I need to get across the border,' he said quickly. 'I need

131

to get away from this country or I will die. Will you get me into the Balkans?'

A hint of danger edged his voice. Rather than making Virginia fearful, it excited her. 'Why will you die? What have you done that makes them want to kill you?'

He shook his head in an effort to add emphasis. 'I upset those people you saw at the station.' He glanced quickly at Raymonde. 'I believe you saw the pig – his name's Corellia. Andreas Corellia. He has a love of big displays, loud speeches, military uniforms. I must get out of the country. Will you help me?'

Virginia glanced at the curling chest hair that sprang from his open shirt. She trembled and did not mind the strong smell of sweat that mingled almost pleasantly with the taste of fear.

'So. What did you do exactly?'

He looked suddenly sheepish. 'I made love to his wife.' He held up his hand almost like a salute. 'But she tempted me! Really she did.'

'And you gave in to temptation. I sense that you like female flesh, Alphonse Ameretti. I sense that a glimpse of a nude belly can halt you in your tracks; can almost get you caught by an army of pursuers in fact.'

Virginia smiled as she said it and reached out to draw imaginary circles in the cluster of chest hairs that peered out so provocatively from his open shirt.

'Will you help me?' he asked, his voice slow and his eyes studying her for the slightest response.

Virginia paused then nodded quickly, almost as if to do otherwise might give her time to change her mind.

'This is going to be dangerous,' Raymonde interjected, his gaze meeting directly with hers. 'A wife is an unassailable chattel as far as an Italian man is concerned. I wonder he hasn't killed you already. Why is that, Alphonse?'

An expression of pride came to the face of the young Italian. 'I run fast. Very fast.'

Both Virginia and Raymonde laughed.

Virginia asked herself what right had she to say yes.

'How do we carry this out?' Her voice seemed very quiet and was directed at no one in particular. There were two more stops before the train crossed the border into the Balkans and made its way to Belgrade. Anything could happen between now and then. Her heart thudded in her chest. How strange that danger can make a man appear even more attractive than he is. How fine the line between sexual arousal and the excitement of fear. She remembered an army officer she had known who had fought in the Great War. She remembered him saying that as he looked down the barrel of his Enfield and saw the enemy approaching, the fear that made his body tremble with anticipation also made him ejaculate at that very moment when he fired the gun. That was how she was feeling now.

'We can't let him shoot you.' She knew she sounded determined. All the same, a smile twitched the corners of her mouth. 'A man who can give a woman such pleasure? Goodness no. We could never allow that to happen.'

It was Raymonde who came up with the solution.

'Alphonse can be your new travelling companion.' With a sigh of exasperation and a sweeping flourish, he pulled the wig of greyish black hair from his head. Alphonse gasped. Unperturbed, Raymonde had a good scratch. 'I doubt that anyone will notice the difference. We're both dark and, anyway, it's you that most people have been noticing, not me.'

Alphonse looked shocked. Obviously he had been fooled by Raymonde's disguise. 'I dress as a woman?' he queried. Fear of looking a fool was now more obvious in his eyes than fear of being shot dead.

'Or get shot for shagging an officer's wife!'

Raymonde exclaimed the last with a swipe at the face powder that lay in smeary patches over his handsome face.

Virginia turned to him. 'But what about you? I can't have

two women in my employ. It's not believable. And I certainly can't have a man here. After all, I still have a mission to accomplish.'

A triumphant kicking off of one heeled shoe was closely followed by the other.

'Bollocks!' he said emphatically.

Virginia raised her eyebrows. 'What?'

'I'm fed up of having cold bollocks. I'm fed up of tottering along on those heels too. Let someone else take a turn. All you have to do is to pay for my ticket. There's a spare cabin next door. I can take that one. I've got enough of my own clothes with me.'

Alphonse was looking a bit agitated, his mouth opening and closing like a goldfish as he tried to slice into the conversation.

Virginia, the valley between her loins trembling as though invisible fingers were laying siege to her clitoris with the most feathery yet electrifying of touches, laid a restraining hand on his shoulder. 'Don't panic, Alphonse.' Her voice trembled. 'I promise you, the time will pass quite quickly and pleasantly. Especially for a man like you who enjoys sexual adventures.' Her most engaging smile seemed to reassure him. She turned back to Raymonde.

'But how do you know the next cabin is empty?'

Raymonde, now stripped down to a pair of silk stockings and green lace garters with a cluster of cherries on the side, smiled ruefully.

His eyes met hers and the tingle in her groin took a jump towards climax. 'One of the attendants told me so. He was trying to get me in there. Dirty old man. I know his sort. I told him I wasn't that sort of girl.'

'No girl,' murmured Alphonse softly as he shook his head. His eyes were as wide as his mouth as a near-naked Raymonde peeled off each stocking, the glistening head of his cock tapping against each thigh as he did so.

'That's for sure,' Virginia added with a wry smirk, her

eyes fixed on the most satisfying penis she had ever had in her life. 'Don't think that,' she warned herself. 'Your future cannot lie with Raymonde.'

Reasons for not helping Alphonse came and went in her mind. 'It's only two more stops in Italy,' she told herself. 'This will all be a great adventure.' Her mind was made up, though she called herself a fool. What about her mission? What about finding a new lover?

'Alright. We'll do that,' she said, nodding her head vigorously so that the sleek line of her shingled hair slid like silk across her cheek. 'Alphonse, you are now my lady travelling companion.'

Alphonse looked from one to the other, his mouth wide open.

Raymonde sprang into action. 'Now that's settled, I'll wash and change. Perhaps you could have some money ready so I can go and buy a ticket. We'd better be quick. It's only half an hour till we leave and head for the border.'

Virginia nodded and sighed all at the same time. 'Yes,' she exclaimed breathlessly, and slumped into a chair. Raymonde peeked out through the curtains.

'There are a few military around, including lover boy. They definitely look as though they're searching for someone.'

'Then you'd better be quick,' warned Virginia.

'Yep!' It was all Raymonde said before he disappeared into the washroom and closed the door behind him.

Alphonse groaned and sank slowly against the wall, head back, eyes closed. His legs lay straight and strong in front of him, hands folded across his waistline.

'A woman,' he moaned to himself. 'The things I do for my country!'

Virginia eyed the lithe body, the tanned bare arms. She tried not to wonder how good they would feel around her. After all, Raymonde was only next door and she had no wish to alienate him, or, dare she say it, upset him.

'I'm getting to the stage,' she thought to herself, 'when I wouldn't want to be without him.' She put the thought away from her mind. After all, this journey was for a purpose. She was here looking for a rich lover, and so far only one target had been tried and tested. Now she was being sidetracked, firstly by this need she had to consider Raymonde's feelings, and now by assisting a fugitive across the border. How did she know he was telling the truth? He could be a criminal, a murderer even, for all she knew.

'No,' she told herself. 'He's a very handsome young man and he has honest eyes.' They were closed at the moment. She guessed he was tired. He started to snore gently.

That was one thing she wasn't going to put up with. She kicked at his foot.

'Alphonse, before you become Dorothy how about making a start and lighting my cigarette. Have one yourself.'

Without her having to tell him where they were, Alphonse opened her bag and got out her cigarette holder.

Their eyes met as he took her packet of Passing Clouds and her gold lighter out of his pocket. He looked sheepish.

'I wasn't going to come originally,' he explained. 'I was going to steal a car and make my way by road. It would have been quite easy. You'd left some money in your bag.'

Virginia eyed him speculatively, the flame from the lighter reflected in his eyes just as surely as it was reflected in hers.

He grinned.

'When I opened your bag I saw the ticket saying Orient Express. I was going to throw it away. Then I smelt your perfume. The inside of your bag, you see, it smelt of you, and when I smelt it, I remembered how you had looked in that doorway.'

His breath quickened. There was a moment of silence between them as his eyes travelled from one coat button to another. He licked his lips and swallowed before he spoke. 'Are you still naked beneath your coat?'

She paused, relishing his moment of apprehension before she nodded.

His voice became softer. 'May I see you?'

Virginia inhaled long and slow on her cigarette. 'Shall I,' she asked herself, 'or shall I turn over a new leaf and allow my body to be seen by no one but a potential rich lover?' It was a ridiculous question. She was a new woman, moulded by emancipation and the new freedom of the nineteen twenties. Important as finding a permanent lover was, there was no rule that said she couldn't indulge herself in little dalliances now and again.

Her eyes viewed him through the smoke before she sighed and took a deep breath. Once she had taken that breath, there was no turning back. His smell was in her, exciting her, bidding her to say yes.

Slowly, with the greatest of deliberation, she put her cigarette to rest on a heavy green ashtray. Then, just as slowly, she got to her feet.

Her eyes held his – almost as if she were challenging him. Starting at her throat, she undid the first button, then the second. The curve of her breasts came into view, full, ripe and proudly jutting forward.

The eyes of the handsome Alphonse followed the hand that next descended. The third and fourth buttons were undone. Her stomach was firm and slightly rounded. Because only one button now remained, the pinkness of her nipples also sprang into view. Alphonse's eyes went from one to the other. She heard his sharp intake of breath. His gaze then fixed on the last button.

Her fingers lingered over it, fondling it, tickling it until, very slowly, she undid it.

This time, Alphonse groaned and his fingers went to his groin. She guessed he was erect, his penis yearning to be free of his trousers and making its way into her. His eyes were now fixed on the nest of wiry black hair that had come into view.

'*Bellissima!*' he murmured, his word coming out like a long, drawn-out sigh.

'There,' she said at last, holding the coat wide but not letting it fall from her shoulders. 'Here I am. Just as when you first saw me.'

His breathing sounded almost pained. His hand still rested over his crotch, his fingers gently caressing what lay behind his buttons.

Although she could not see any visible movement in his trousers, she knew all the same that it was there. His heart rate would be increasing as more blood was pumped down into his loins. As the blood spun with dizzying rapidity into Alphonse's lower body, his penis would be hardening and the first emissions would be seeping like translucent pearls from its tip. And all because his eyes were staring at her naked body. It was as though she were a plate of food and he was a man who had been hungry for a fortnight.

There was something intangibly pleasant about standing there before him like some carved and beautiful statue. It made her feel as though she were something truly precious, of extraordinary worth. Such a feeling excited her.

She was aware of her nipples standing out from her heaving breasts, as though they had been carved from chips of stone. She was also aware that she was still sticky between her legs, and was reminded that one man had already had her today. Somehow, she did not want Alphonse to know that.

'Do you like what you see?' she asked softly.

He nodded. 'Very much. Would you let me—'

'No. If you mean will I let you fuck me, then I have to say no. But there is something I would like you to do.'

His disappointment at her refusal remained on his face, but he did eventually nod his agreement.

'Whatever you want me to do, I will do.'

His answer pleased her. 'What a difference between this man and the one who has just had me,' she thought to herself.

Delicious shivers ran over her cool flesh as she considered what she wanted this man to do to her. It seemed incredibly dangerous, incredibly wicked. It also seemed oddly perverted.

She took a deep breath. 'Do you still have your gun?'

He nodded. 'Yes. I do.'

'Then . . .' she started slowly . . . 'run it over me like you did back in the piazza.' There. It was out.

His eyes widened in amazement. His breath quickened as he reached with a slow, trembling hand into his belt and just as slowly brought out his revolver.

There it was in his hand. Cold, dark and deadly.

'It's not loaded,' he whispered gently.

'Good.'

Virginia gazed into his eyes, willing him to do as she had requested. She gave a little cry as the cool metal touched her shoulder then ran gently over one breast, then the other.

Resting one hand on her hip as if to steady her, he let the hand holding the gun trail over her flesh. All the while his eyes held hers and she took in his smell, the bristles on his chin, the shape of his mouth.

She sighed and ripples of pleasure seemed to seep beneath the surface of her skin, leaving small shivers trembling in their wake.

So engrossed was she in what he was doing and what she herself was feeling, that she hardly noticed that Raymonde was standing in the open doorway to the white enamelled washroom.

It was a though he'd been frozen to the spot.

For a moment he seemed to have difficulty finding his voice. 'I'm off to get a ticket.' He said it quickly. 'It's not too long till this train shoves off.'

As he brushed past her, Virginia inhaled the smell of him. It was similar to that of Alphonse, but different, his masculine scent mixed with a fresh soapiness. A surge of erotic sensations ran swiftly through her. She had an urge to press her lips to his bare chest, but could see he was in no mood to loiter for her benefit.

Swiftly, Alphonse shoved the gun back into his waistband.

Slowly Virginia wrapped her coat back around herself, but she did not rebutton it.

Silently, they both watched Raymonde dress in male attire.

Virginia was strangely stirred by seeing him slide his legs into his underwear, then his trousers. He was grim faced as he buttoned his shirt, his eyes looking at her with a hint of accusation.

Her fingers moved nervously against her coat as she watched him trying to fasten his shirt collar in place.

'You look good in those clothes,' she said lightly. 'Better than you did in that dress.'

'No doubt,' he snapped.

Suddenly, Virginia felt strangely guilty.

'But why should I?' she thought. 'I'm my own woman. He's only a servant, a barman I picked up in Paris.' But still she was troubled.

She made another effort. 'Will a Thomas Cook do?'

He was putting on his jacket but paused to look at her with puzzlement rather than anger, or jealousy, or whatever it was he was feeling.

Virginia shrugged and reached for the drawer where she kept the crocodile-skin case that held her travel documents. 'These,' she said holding up a slim sheaf of papers. 'Travellers cheques they call them. I'll sign a few then you've got—'

'I need cash. I'm a new passenger. We don't know each other, do we.'

There was accusation in his eyes.

Virginia tried not to look or sound deflated. 'Of course. Of course. You're right, Raymonde.' She put the travellers cheques away and went to her handbag. She looked questioningly at Alphonse.

'It's still there.' He gave her the same rueful grin that he had before.

Virginia took out a wad of lire and held them out to Raymonde.

'Take this. It should be enough.'

She took small comfort from the fact that his fingers brushed against hers. It was such a slight action. So brief. She stepped back from him as though she had been burned.

Once he was fully dressed in pale tan day suit, white shirt, silk tie and tan shoes, Raymonde picked up a trilby and fixed it on his head. It sloped slightly to the left side.

It would look better tilting to the other side, Virginia thought to herself. Her fingers curled into her palms as the urge to adjust it grew stronger. Once she had done it, she would have to take hold of his neck and seek his lips. But she didn't do that. He looked too serious.

'Just as well,' said that mercenary voice that lived in her head. 'Raymonde is not rich. He is merely handsome.' But there was another voice too that lived side by side with the more mercentary part of her nature. The other voice told her that Raymonde was also the most desirable man she had ever met. She suddenly decided to take the plunge.

'Raymonde, I think I should . . .'

He took a quick step backwards.

'I won't be a moment.' His voice sounded like a warning.

It pained her that he did not look in her direction before going out of the door.

Virginia stared at it once it had closed. There was a tightness in her chest. 'Forget it,' she told herself. 'He's just a waiter you met in a French hotel. Nothing more. Nothing less.' All the same, her lips trembled.

Silk lining against her body begged attention. Alphonse

was gently massaging her lower back and upper buttocks. It was a pleasant feeling.

'He loves you,' he said simply. 'Do you love him?'

Virginia looked up at him and wondered why she couldn't respond. In her mind she answered. The smell of him was still there. So was the sight of him slipping out of his dressing gown. Strangely enough, Raymonde dressed had stirred her more strongly than him naked. It was as if the sex had been superseded by the sight of the man as presented to the world.

'Control yourself,' said that mercenary voice again. So she took a deep breath and smiled as if she didn't have a care in the world. After all, she could still go after Davis Sedglingham if she wanted. Yet he no longer looked her way, and when he did he only smiled. Not once had he invited her to dine with him or to visit his cabin. Why was that? she wondered.

Letting her coat at last slide from her shoulders, she reached for her cigarette holder. Smoke still rose from the half-smoked Passing Cloud, though the ash was now halfway down its length.

As she picked it up, the ash dropped onto the table.

'Damn!' she exclaimed.

'It's only ash,' Alphonse remarked, taking a step closer to her.

Virginia turned her back on him. 'No,' she said quietly. 'It isn't only ash that seems to be falling. That's the trouble.'

Everything went according to plan. No one questioned the handsome young Englishman buying a ticket to Istanbul. The military only gave him a passing glance. Even the officer in charge did not let his gaze linger on him too long. After all, the sight of the man who had violated his wife was etched indelibly in his mind. Especially his backside. It was his backside he had seen as he had entered the bedroom to

142

find both of them naked. But he also remembered his face, and although his face was similar to that of Raymonde, it did not seem so to Lieutenant Andreas Corellia. The reason was rage. Perhaps if he had not felt such rage he would have noticed that the features of Virginia Vernon's travelling companion had altered a little. He noticed nothing.

So the Orient Express pulled out of Milan watched by those who were left behind.

The lieutenant narrowed his eyes as he watched it disappear. He very much wanted to see Alphonse Ameretti again but he didn't know where he was. He would also like to see Virginia Vernon again and he knew she was still on the train.

As is the way of providence, Corellia bumped into a telegraph messenger on his way to his car. The messenger's bicycle clattered to the floor along with its rider.

'Bumbling fool!' exclaimed Corellia. 'What the devil do you think you are doing!'

'Sorry. So sorry,' muttered the scrawny young man as he scrambled to his feet. He held up one grubby hand containing a brown envelope. 'I have a message for someone on the train.'

'Well you've missed it!' the lieutenant's voice had lost none of its anger. 'So that is that, you stupid man. Now what are you going to do?'

His face was level with the man now. The latter had picked himself up and was doing his best not to blink as the officer's spittle landed on his face.

'I will have to go back to the operator and get him to send it on further down the wire,' he said in a small, pitiful voice.

'Then go and do it. Now!'

Corellia's voice was so loud it must have echoed all round the poor man's brain. His head seemed to slide back on his neck as if it were trying to retreat down into his collar.

'Yes. Yes. I will do that.'

He reached for his bike.

Corellia dived for the back of his neck and held the scrawny object as though it were merely the gizzard of chicken.

'Tell me who the telegram is for.'

The messenger's eyes bulged. He licked his lips. There was a mite of defiance in him yet. 'I am not supposed to give—'

Corellia's grip tightened. 'Tell me!'

The messenger raised the envelope so it was immediately between him and Corellia.

'Miss Virginia Vernon,' he pronounced, then flopped into a heap as Corellia let him go.

Chapter 17

On the first evening of their rearranged subterfuge, Virginia Vernon and her travelling companion, Miss Dorothy Plumber, attracted no more attention than before. Primarily, this was because Alphonse was very similar in both stature and looks to Raymonde. It was also because most eyes tended to rest on Virginia and not really notice what Miss Plumber was like.

Davis Sedglingham caught Virginia's eye. She waved to him. He paused and for a moment looked as if he were about to retreat. Zweizer and his wife appeared behind him and blocked his escape. Virginia thought she saw some unspoken acknowledgement pass between the two men. She put the idea to one side once she could see that Davis had no option but to come her way.

He halted by her table. She took a deep breath and felt her flesh responding to the seductive mix of tobacco and eau de cologne that wafted over her with the slightest move he made.

'Davis,' she said in her most alluring voice, 'I've seen so little of you. Are you avoiding me, you naughty boy?'

He smiled a different smile from the one he used when he had been intent on seducing her. 'Indeed no, Virginia. I will fit you into my schedule whenever I can.'

Virginia tried not to bite too hard on her cigarette holder. Ebony didn't come cheap and neither did she. 'Your schedule?'

He nodded curtly. 'I'm a busy man, Virginia. I have

many concerns on my mind. Responsibilities weigh rather heavy at the present time. To start with, I have a problem with my servant, Mario. You must excuse me.'

A dining-car attendant came with an invitation for him to join Herr and Frau Zweizer at their table.

He bid her a formal goodnight and went back the way he had come. She watched him go. It still rankled that he had not sought her out since that first night together, yet she had expected him to. What responsibilities weighed so heavy that he no longer had any time for her?

She saw the Swiss banker get up and shake hands with him as he approached. Frau Zweizer lifted her hand to be kissed. For a moment, Virginia was almost sure she saw the dull eyes sparkle and the lipstick-hard mouth gain a warmth it never usually had.

It was hard to swallow her pride, but swallow it she must. 'Never mind,' she told herself as she tossed her head and looked in a predatory way around the dining car. 'There are other fish in the sea.' And indeed there were. Other men were glancing her way. Strangely enough, she hardly noticed them. They seemed like mere blobs of whitish, pinkish greyness; without eyes, without noses, in fact, without features of any sort. Her eyes kept returning to one man in particular, one man who looked even more irresistible dressed as a rich man than he had as a poor one.

Raymonde, who was now attired in a similar fashion to most other male passengers, was attracting the attention of a number of women.

'Is Raymonde alright?' asked a concerned Alphonse, his voice cracking as he fought to feminize it.

'Yes.' With guilty abruptness, Virginia turned her gaze to the passing scenery. 'I'm not jealous,' she told herself. 'I'm not jealous at all.' Her eyes slid back in Raymonde's direction. A trim woman, who was most definitely on the wrong side of forty, was paying attention to him. Judging by the tangerine organza outfit she was wearing, and the glinting of diamonds and gold, she was just as obviously wealthy. She had stopped to talk to Raymonde and was now sitting herself on the chair opposite him.

'She's almost old enough to be his mother,' Virginia muttered under her breath.

Alphonse raised his eyebrows. 'Eh?'

Virginia shook her head. 'Nothing.' She took a taste of her wine. It was dark red and trickled like plum juice over her tongue. One taste was not enough. She took another, then another.

A puzzled expression came to the face of the good-looking Alphonse. He leaned forward. She could tell he was about to ask a question.

'Can you tell me, Miss Virginia. Why do English ladies wear no knickers?'

His face was a picture of puzzled innocence.

Virginia covered her mouth with her hand to stop from laughing out loud.

This only made Alphonse look more puzzled.

Virginia let her hand fall. A smile remained.

'Let me show you,' she said softly.

'Just as she had with Raymonde, she slid her foot out of her shoe and pushed it up under Alphonse's dress.

He gasped.

'Miss Virginia!'

'Shhh,' she hissed. 'Just enjoy it.'

'Oh, I will,' he breathed as he sank back in his chair, bliss written all over his face.

Beneath her stockinged toes, Virginia felt the spongy softness of his scrotal sac. As her foot travelled on, softness was replaced by hardness. Alphonse had a worthwhile erection and it was growing by the second. It was a most pleasant diversion to the angst she was feeling.

Alphonse lay his head against the back of his seat. He half closed his eyes and small moans of delight seeped like sighs from between his lips.

Virginia's spirits had lightened, but every so often her gaze went back to Raymonde. He appeared to be in deep conversation with the woman. Their heads seemed to get closer and closer.

What would they do next?

Her question was answered pretty quickly.

Following a light trill of feminine laughter, they got up from their seats. With his arm circling the woman's waist, and her glancing every so often up into his face, Raymonde and the woman left the dining car.

So intense was Virginia's attention towards the departing pair, that she barely noticed the warm fluid cascading over her stockinged foot or the low, almost strangulated sigh from the lips of the man opposite her.

Venice was golden. At least, that was the way it seemed to Agnetha Zweizer.

'Hans. You never fail me,' she said softly as he helped her to settle on the crimson silk seat of the gondola.

'My darling Agnetha, how could I when I love you so much. How many times do I have to tell you that I dream of you day and night. Do I not prove it by crossing Europe to see you?'

She watched him make his way to the rear of the vessel, his thigh muscles seeming to thrust for freedom against the dark tightness of his trousers, the shape of his buttocks so obvious and so enticing.

Her sigh was one of impatience. Her look was that of pure lust. 'A gondolier's outfit suits you very well, Hans. You really are a fine figure of a man.'

Hans smiled down at her as he unhitched from a red and white striped pole which he dipped into the greyish green of the water. 'I'm glad you think so, Agnetha. But then, what can you expect. A fine figure of a woman deserves a fine figure of a man. Any less would be an insult.'

She laughed at that and turned back to face the front, her

cheeks as pink as that of an innocent young girl.

'Just relax and enjoy your journey, lady. Enjoy Venice.'

'I will,' she murmured. 'I most certainly will.'

She settled back on the crimson cushions and would have trailed her hand through the dark waters of the canal if it hadn't been for the many warnings she'd heard about the diseases that could be caught from it.

Instead, she consoled herself – if console was the right word – by studying the faded yet beautiful visage of many an ancient palace.

To her it felt as though she were gliding through the centuries and not just through the water. Byzantine facades dating from the thirteenth century were replaced by the more elaborate medieval Venetian, their walls a mass of white, blue and terracotta tiles. In turn, these buildings gave way to the more ornate deliberations of Baroque and thence to the clean lines and Corinthian columns of the neo-Classical.

Agnetha shivered with apprehension. Soon, all this would be no more than a painted scene is to a theatre. Soon, she would be a part of a performance as old as the human race itself. Like Eve she had been tempted. She had bitten of forbidden fruit and she wanted more of it.

Back in Milan, Hans had taken her to a room that seemed to be all mirrors, glittering candelabra and gilded statues.

After disrobing her, he had lain her on a coverlet of rich brocade. Her head had rested on pillows scented with the most flowery of perfumes.

'Lie here and I will give you pleasure.'

Feeling like an adored goddess, she did as he said, arms wide and legs spread open.

Soon, she had felt his hands on her toes, up over her feet and around her ankles. She had smelt the sweetness of almond oil and had murmured with pleasure as the slipperiness of his hands had swept up over her legs.

Soft sounds had escaped her throat as his hands had gone higher, his lips kissing her knees and the white skin of her inner thighs. Her flesh had trembled.

His hands had travelled further. So had his mouth. At first, she could only feel his breath gently rustling her pubic hair, its touch delicate but still enough to set her body juices flowing.

By the time his tongue slid between her nether lips, her hips were rising to meet him and she was groaning in ecstasy.

Delicious shivers ran through her as his tongue at last tapped at her clitoris. 'It's like a little button,' she thought, 'like the ones you get in a lift.'

And like a lift, she seemed to zoom upwards, or at least the sensations she was experiencing did. Pleasure spread over her. She cried out as his tongue slid further among her fleshy lips and dipped gently into her vagina. She had wriggled her hips in open invitation that he could and should do more.

'Enough!'

There was a need to shout that word only once. Hans knew exactly what to do. His tongue had gone back to where it was truly required. She had arched her body as powerful sensations spread from her pulsing button. His tongue licked it, tapped it and, as it did so, his lips had sucked on her until she had felt she was being sucked into his mouth.

Orgasm after orgasm had coursed through her body as, dutiful slave that he was, Hans had brought her off merely with the aid of his tongue.

After that, he had poured wine and, again, Agnetha had asked him why he never took his clothes off, why he never wanted to fuck her.

Wineglass in hand, they had sat gazing into each other's eyes. Again he had explained what he had explained a dozen times before.

'My love is for you, my dear lady. My own needs do not count. All you require of me is my tongue. I do exactly what you want me to do, do I not?'

Sighing happily, she had stroked his mouth, her eyes full of wonder as his tongue had poked through his lips, a lengthy virile thing, menacing in its power, delicate in its touch.

'I'm so glad you don't want me to do . . .' she had paused until finding the courage to say it ' . . . those other things. I think I have found a marvel in you, and for that I am truly grateful.'

That had been Milan, and this was Venice. Glorious as its sights and its history was, Agnetha was looking forward to sampling its delights in a different way.

'This is it,' she heard Hans say. A thrill of excitement ran through her. Soon she would be drifting into Paradise as Hans, her beloved, licked her to distraction. In an effort to subdue her inflamed passions, she made a concerted effort to take notice of where they were going.

The prow of the shiny black gondola turned and nudged its nose into a narrow inlet between two buildings whose gaunt shadows allowed no sunlight to play on the chill, dark water.

Agnetha shivered as they left the blessing of sunlight and entered the dark shadows. Such shivers joined with the ones she was already experiencing due to sexual excitement. But it was harder here to immerse her thoughts in her surroundings. This inlet was nowhere near as beautiful as the canal they had lately left behind them.

Trails of green moss hung from the crumbling stonework up to and a foot or two beyond eye level. She started at the close-by sound of a rat entering the water.

Hans turned the boat so that they were berthed broad side on to a set of wet stone steps that led from the canal and up to a small quay outside a narrow building.

Agnetha waited until he had tied up and was on the steps, arms outstretched, to help her off.

His hand touched hers and she took it.

'My darling,' he whispered. She barely had time to make the steps before his lips were on hers. Her heart skipped a beat. What a man Hans was, and what a lucky woman she was to have someone like him to make her feel good.

'What is this place?' He kissed her throat as she tilted her head back to gaze up at the lofty walls that bounded them on three sides.

'It's a palace,' he said softly. 'A Venetian palace fit for a queen.'

Agnetha did her best to hold him at arms' length, but her elbows were still bent. Hans was so big. So strong.

'How could you afford to rent a place like this?' she asked him. 'After all, you're only a chauffeur.'

Still smiling, he shook his head then took hold of her chin.

'Like lots of men, women too, I have secrets. So don't ask. Just accept. And enjoy everything I give you.'

Enjoy was exactly what she did. He held her tightly to him. It was just as well. She could feel her knees buckling as his lips covered hers. She wanted to faint away entirely as the biggest and best tongue she had ever known entered her mouth. Soon it would be doing other things, things her husband had long ago stopped doing.

Raymonde too had taken a gondola. He had been about to step on it with his new acquaintance, a Mrs Rosalie Newton Thurbird, whose late husband, so she said, had left her a fortune. Just as they had settled into their seats, bodies and thighs pressing comfortably together, Virginia had come running up, the new Dorothy, or rather Alphonse, tottering along behind her.

Raymonde gave him a quick smile. It was amazing how alike they were. Thank God, he thought to himself, that it's him in the high heels and not me.

'Can we join you?' Virginia said as she pressed a few more lire into the wide palm of the grateful gondolier.

She hadn't waited for an answer.

'Well this is nice,' she had beamed once Alphonse was sat safely beside her. 'Are you going to introduce us?' Her smile remained fixed. Her eyes glittered with half-disguised acrimony at the lady with a liking for tangerine.

And so, following all the introductions and Rosalie's remark that her husband was fully titled Albert Alfred Thurbird the Third, the gondola shoved off.

Virginia pretended to be interested in the buildings they passed. Inside she was trying to control the jealousy she was feeling.

If Davis had asked her to join him, she would have, but he still seemed unduly evasive. He also seemed to have acquired a new 'bosom buddy'. He and Heinrich Zweizer were spending a lot of time together. She had seen both of them race down to where the gondolas were berthed way ahead of anyone else. She had no idea where they were going or what they would be doing and no longer cared. But the fact that Raymonde seemed to be avoiding her made her want to be with him all the more – and she felt ashamed of feeling like that.

Raymonde was enjoying himself. He knew perfectly well that Virginia was feeling jealous and he wanted her to go on feeling that way. Then she might understand how he had felt when he'd seen Alphonse running that gun over her body. Perhaps he shouldn't feel like that, seeing as she was in effect his employer. But he couldn't help it. Stumbling in on them had upset him. Somehow, he craved involvement in her seductions – just like when he had watched her seduce Davis Sedglingham.

Of course, Sedglingham hadn't known Raymonde was watching. Virginia had thought it a wise precaution that he should. So there he had been, peeping through a set of louvred doors, his penis pulsing in his hand and ready for her once Davis had gone.

It was the best sex they had ever had. They had both agreed on that. Somehow, him being involved in her seduction had overruled any feelings of jealousy. Now he was cursing himself that he hadn't handed Alphonse over to the authorities. But it was too late now.

In the meantime, Rosalie was very good company and her experience certainly showed up in bed.

His new companion was a woman who sought to do everything possible to keep a man interested. If she thought that sucking on his cock for half the night was just the thing to keep him on the boil, that was certainly what she would do. In fact, it was exactly what she did do.

'I think,' he had thought to himself as he lay there, 'that the perfect woman is one who can go on sucking for a hundred years whilst I just lie here and enjoy it.'

'Isn't Rosalie just great,' he said smiling and taking Rosalie's hand in his.

Virginia didn't flinch. 'Marvellous,' she replied with all the insincerity she could muster. 'Especially for her age. How many children do you have, Rosalie?'

Rosalie's well-painted expression did not falter. 'Two sons. Both at Harvard.'

Alphonse pretended he wasn't listening. It was as though history was his subject and he was devouring it with unfettered enthusiasm. His gaze raked the buildings that lined the edge of the canal. Something suddenly caught his eye.

There was a deep inlet between two particular buildings. A gondola was moored in the shadows there, its outline only slightly blacker than the shadows themselves. A gondolier and a woman were embracing. The woman was familiar. Did he know her? Then it came to him. She was a fellow passenger on the Orient Express and the man she was with was not her husband.

Chapter 18

Both Herr Zweizer and Davis Sedglingham had waited until virtually all the other passengers had left the train before doing so themselves. Even then, they had left separately as though the last thing they wanted was company of any sort.

As they left, Davis nodded politely at the two Greeks, whereas Zweizer barely managed a thin smile and spoke no greeting at all, showing how different in character the two men were.

Eventually, as the buzz of the city morning mellowed into the idle hum of the afternoon, they met up as arranged.

Together they sat at a cafe table in a less fashionable part of Venice where few tourists ever ventured.

Heads almost meeting over a slatted wooden table beneath a sweet-smelling lemon tree, they drank French brandy. The spot they sat in was spangled by a continuous kaleidoscope of sunlight and shade that altered in pattern each time the breeze rustled through the overhead branches.

Davis called for more brandy.

The waiter, who was also the patron of the establishment, ambled out from the darker recesses of the cafe, his face shiny with sweat. A red network of veins etched the end of his bulbous nose. Judging by the appearance of his face, this was a man who not only sold sizeable quantities of spirit, but imbibed it as well. Beneath the large, red protuberance hung a dense black moustache that completely hid his mouth. There was less hair on his head.

As the man refilled their glasses with fingers as thick as the salami that hung smoking in the dark cafe, Davis exchanged a knowing look with Herr Zweizer.

'Patron,' he said, without looking up at the man who continued to pour a good measure of amber liquid into his glass, 'as you may possibly have judged, we are gentlemen of the world and, as such, have an appetite for all things – shall we say – worldly.'

He gave the man a sudden, knowing look. It was followed by an equally knowing wink.

Zweizer rested both hands on his cane and leaned forward, his expression a blend of apprehension and excitement.

The patron's dark eyes held those of the fair-skinned, fair-haired Englishman.

'Does this man understand?' whispered Zweizer from across the table.

'Oh, yes,' Davis replied with a curt nod, though his eyes did not leave those of the pink-faced Italian. 'He understands alright.'

The man nodded. '*Si*. I understand. You want whorehouse.'

'Ah!' exclaimed Davis, then held up his finger in warning. 'Yes, we do want such an establishment, but we want the very best, the most expensive, the most adventurous. Do you know of such a place?'

The patron nodded then held up his finger as if bidding them to wait.

He ambled back into the darkness of his cafe. A few minutes passed before he returned with another man whose appearance alarmed rather than amazed the two men at the table. The man was tall and thin, his cheeks sunken, his hair mere wisps of grey fuzz that hinted it might once have been blond. His eyes were blue and, although they were bright, there was a certain kind of brittleness about the way they glittered.

A white linen jacket was worn casually over baggy white trousers. It was the sort of suit worn in the tropics by rubber or tobacco planters. Smudges of stain decorated the lapels and it had obviously not been ironed for some considerable time.

The man's eyes betrayed a hint of scorn as he lifted a battered Panama from his head.

Both Sedglingham and Zweizer looked down their noses in his direction though they were both still sitting down. Their contempt seemed to pass unnoticed. The man leered and exposed yellow-stained teeth.

'Hi. I hear you guys want some action. Is that right?'

Davis and Zweizer rose from their seats.

'You're English?' David exclaimed.

The man grinned. 'No, you are, and you're jumping to conclusions. Name's Lawford Parkinson. Born in Louisiana, citizen of the world. I'm a man who has an intimate knowledge of every den of inequity from here to Rangoon and Canton. How d'ya do.'

Davis, then Zweizer offered their hands. Parkinson brushed by without returning the courtesy, his head held high in a way that suggested arrogance.

'Well come on, men,' he called over his shoulder. 'If you're hard in your pants and looking for action, let's get going or you'll be past it before you know it.'

Without negotiation about whether he wanted payment or whether they wanted another drink before leaving, Parkinson sauntered off. Hands in pockets and whistling Dixie, he swaggered at a leisurely and rather ungainly gait, hat tilted forward; perhaps to shield his eyes from the strong sunlight, or more likely because he was in no fit state to place it in a more agreeable position.

'Papa?'

Davis and Zweizer merely glanced at the young woman who had come to the door. For her part, she paid them even less attention. With a worried frown she watched the white-suited man swagger off, the Englishman striding and the Swiss puffing to catch up with him.

The patron appeared beside her, his hand upon her arm. 'We cannot choose our relatives, Maria,' he said softly, and the girl looked crestfallen.

Even after they had disappeared from view, the girl stood there. So immersed was she in her own thoughts, that she did not pay any attention to the sound of footsteps.

'I'd like coffee if I may.'

Disturbed from her reverie, she started. Turning, she gazed into the eyes of a man wearing expensive, though slightly flashy clothes. There was a hard look in his eyes and a small scar on his cheek. His accent was similar to that of her father, yet broader and far more harsh.

Al Hutchinson let his eyes stay on the girl for a while. She was pleasant to look at, but not his type. Anyway, his mind was elsewhere at the moment. He had business to attend to, but it wasn't business that was riling him at the moment. Petula was the problem. She was less compliant with his sexual demands at the moment. He had already made up his mind to replace her the minute he got back to New York.

In the meantime, he had a sore need in his trousers and there was only one woman on the train he was interested in. She was English and her name was Virginia Vernon. He'd found out that much. So far he had not approached her. 'Hell,' he thought to himself, 'just cos she's a classy dame, don't mean to say she ain't partial to a bit of monkey business.'

But Al was basically a simple guy, and although he could handle a gun or a moll like Petula with ease and run rings around the police chief back in New York, he felt like a high-school kid in the company of someone like Virginia Vernon.

What would it be like he wondered, to have her bend over for him the same way Petula did. My, but that would really be an achievement. Just imagine, he thought to himself, how firm and white her young backside would be, how tightly her buttocks would clench as he dragged his fingernails across them, his fingers determinedly jabbing between her cheeks and into her body.

Somehow he knew he was fooling himself. He had a fear within that he would go weak in her presence. Despite the warm air of a Venetian day, a shiver ran down his back. 'Don't be a fool,' he warned. 'Be a man. Be your usual self.'

But events interceded in the simple masculine world that Al inhabited. As in Milan, he had done his business for the day, but even his hard veneer was cracked by the atmosphere of the ancient city. He had wanted to go sightseeing and had told his business associates that this was so. They had been generous to hail a gondola for his pleasure. From the water he had seen all he had wanted, then had asked the gondolier to set him down near a place where there weren't any crazy tourists to disturb his thinking process. Alone he had expected to remain. The last thing he had expected was to see the object of his desire come tripping around the corner. Like him, she was also alone. Her eyes were downcast and so were the ends of her pretty lips. Her arms were crossed in front of her and her footsteps had a certain kind of sharpness about them.

The deep blue of her eyes met his. And suddenly Al was a small boy gazing in Maceys window and longing for a tin pedal car that was in there. Of course, he never had got the pedal car, but if he played his cards right . . .

Virginia smiled, and at the same time she wondered why she hadn't thought to seduce him sooner. There was no doubt that he had money. There was also no doubt that he was a very good-looking man; shorter than Raymonde, more stocky, but still attractive in a dangerous, wild kind of way.

'Well, hello,' she called, and waved her hand. At the same time, she wondered where his woman friend was. His moll. Wasn't that the word?

'Miss Vernon.' He rose slowly from his chair. 'I . . . I'm

just having some coffee. Would you care to join me?'

Raymonde and his teasing was forgotten. So was her disappointment that Davis seemed no longer to be interested. 'But this man,' she thought to herself, 'this twentieth-century bandit from the New World *is* interested in me.' By the looks of him, she could very well get more interested herself.

Virginia smiled and walked straight towards him. 'Delighted,' she said. His hands shook as he pulled a chair out for her. Virginia noticed this. Her eyes followed him as he went to the cafe door and called for more coffee, then sat down. He tried to talk, but at first all that came out was the clearing of his throat.

Virginia took the initiative. 'Are you from New York?' She already knew the answer.

'Yeah! Yeah. How did you guess?'

She shrugged as she took out her cigarette holder. 'That's all it was. Just a guess.'

Al's hand was still trembling when he offered her a light. He shivered a little when she placed her own fingers on him to hold him steady.

Again he became the nervous young boy out on his first date.

'It's very nice here,' said Virginia, looking round her as though they were sitting in St Mark's Square and not in a small alley where a lemon tree grew out of a crack in the wall. 'I'm rather glad I found it. It's so nice to get away from everyone, don't you think?' He only nodded and mumbled a rushed yes.

She eyed him speculatively. Could this be the lover she was looking for? She took a deep breath as if the air she breathed was also her resolve. With a quick, furtive look she assessed what this man might be like unclothed and in bed. Vigorous, she decided. She already knew he was rich. 'Could I possibly live in New York and have a gangster as a lover?' she asked herself.

The thought amused her, though she tried not to show it. The awkward silence between them persisted. This New York tough guy was having enough trouble trying to find his tongue as it was.

Her gaze wandered to the leaves above and from that to a passing woman clad completely in black and carrying a heavily laden basket. She left it to him to find his voice.

'Did you get separated from your friend?' he managed to ask at last.

'Gladly!' she exclaimed, turning to him, her eyes bright with amusement. 'I wanted to be alone. Why would I want to be with another woman all the time?'

She didn't tell him that she'd stalked off because Raymonde was paying too much attention to that widow woman he'd picked up and that Alphonse was talking to the American woman as though he really was a woman himself.

'You prefer men?' Al asked cautiously.

Virginia assessed that an opinion was beginning to form that she was a woman just like any other.

She smiled sweetly and nodded from behind a pall of fine blue smoke.

'Oh, yes,' she said in a soft, low voice. 'I definitely prefer men.'

He saw her wriggle slightly and wondered if she had suddenly become uncomfortable. He was about to ask if she'd like to go for a walk when the touch of her foot stopped him in his tracks.

He gasped. 'That's your foot,' he said in a half-strangled manner. 'You're rubbing my balls with your foot . . . well I'll be . . .'

'So be it,' thought Virginia with reformed resolution. 'If Raymonde and Alphonse are so wrapped up with that widow, it does give me time to concentrate on the real reason for this journey. Anyway, this guy is loaded.' She could tell that just by looking at his tie pin and the three rings on each hand.

Al licked at his lips. The unease that had been in his eyes disappeared.

'Would you like to go somewhere?' he asked huskily. 'I'd rather not come in my pants.'

Virginia paused and gave him the most coquettish look ever, then smiled slowly.

'I think I would like a long, slow ride in a gondola.' She stressed the word 'ride' in such a provocative way that he could not possibly misunderstand exactly what she wanted.

They did just that, only this was not one of the more ordinary ones that ply forever up and down the Grand Canal, ferrying tourists from one end to the other. This was the sort with a palanquin set in dead centre and crimson curtains that could be pulled around for privacy.

Al threw a wad of notes at a very grateful gondolier. 'Two hours,' he snarled, and the gondolier was in no doubt that there was no cheating this particular passenger.

Curtained from the outside world, Virginia lay on red cushions and watched as her potential lover got himself comfortable.

Al slipped his jacket from his shoulders, then undid the leather holster that held his gun.

Virginia trembled as she watched him place it to one side. Here again was that feeling of danger that could so enhance the desire she felt.

Once he was down to only his shirt and his trousers, he pressed himself against her and she could feel the warmth of his flesh. His hands caressed her, stroking her hair and her face as his lips crushed hers until she could barely breathe.

As his mouth explored her lips, his hands explored her body. Each breast fitted perfectly into each great hand. She moaned when he squeezed them and murmured in ecstasy as his hands wandered up beneath the green knitted skirt she wore.

His fingers rasped against her stockings. She could feel tingles of desire starting around the small pink button that

162

lay so secretly yet so obviously between her legs.

The heat of his breath was against her ear as his hand found her garters and the soft flesh above it.

She heard him gasp and her senses seemed to whirl in dizzy response.

Slowly, his fingers travelled beneath the silky softness of her camiknickers and found the superior silkiness of her pubic hair.

She moaned as he tangled her curls around his fingers before probing further and coaxing her legs apart. One finger slid into the warm crease of her divide. One hand remained on her breast, kneading, pressing, squeezing and playing with it. His mouth nipped at her throat then went down to suck at her nipples through the soft wool of her dress.

She cried out as that single, exploratory finger slid through her labia and dipped without pause into her vagina.

'I must have you,' she sighed against his face. 'I must.'

She heard him laugh. He took hold of her hand and placed it on his crotch. Virginia moaned as though she were a child who has just been shown the biggest chocolate bar in the shop. It was something like that. His penis was hard and the size of it gave birth to an intense curiosity within her. She had to see this thing she could feel moving beneath her fingers.

'Go on, Ginny,' she heard him gasp. 'Unbutton me and get it out. See what a big one I've got for you.'

Whether he was teasing or not, Virginia was mad keen to get his penis out of his trousers.

With trembling fingers, she undid his buttons and slid her hand through the opening at the front of his underpants. What she felt there made her gasp. Not only was Al's penis hard and hot, it was of such a size that was bound to fill and satisfy. A single drop of fluid glistened at the end of it and trembled each time his penis jerked in her hand. Just touching it made her want it in any way she could have it. For the first time in a week, Raymonde and his lovemaking was driven from her mind.

All the same, Virginia did notice that Al was watching her with something akin to trepidation. It was almost as though he was not entirely sure that he was pleasing her.

This, she decided, was something new. This man had advocated control of the situation to her. This was indeed a red-letter day. She herself was in complete control.

Delicious sensations were flowing through her body. For the moment the fact that Al Hutchinson could not really be a contender for her long-term affections didn't seem to matter. Of course she could consider going to New York, but then . . . did she really want to hitch herself up with a man who might get shot by a rival or a cop at any moment?

No, she told herself, she did not. She would enjoy this for what it was, a sexual adventure.

She made a faint mewing sound as she looked at him, then, easing her dress up around her hips, she lifted her buttocks from the cushions and opened her legs wide.

Al's eyes looked as though they might pop out of his head. He groaned and the penis Virginia held in her hand jerked in response. A small seepage of fluid oozed from its end like a single tear drop. Virginia bent her head and licked it off, but not too quickly. She deliberated over it and ran her tongue around it before taking it totally into her mouth.

'Do you like it?' she asked him, her voice as warm and slick as treacle.

He swallowed, managed to nod.

'Then kiss me, you dog! Kiss me between my legs!'

Grabbing a handful of his hair, she pulled him down towards her lap. Would he do as she ordered? She was pretty sure he would. He gasped, but did not protest.

Congratulating herself for having judged him correctly, Virginia lay her head back on the pillows and closed her eyes. Still holding onto his hair so she could manipulate his head as she wished, she sighed as his nose came into contact with her clitoris and his tongue licked at her exposed labia.

To him, her sex would appear pink, moist and smelling delicately of arousal.

Earlier she had experienced sexual excitement resulting from the hint of danger that Alphonse had brought with him. Now she was experiencing heightened sexual excitement because she was in control of a man.

Moans of pleasure passed through her lips and the sounds she made were in time with pulling his head back and forth upon her.

'Give me more tongue,' she demanded, and he did.

'Poke the tip of it onto that hard little button,' she went on. 'Ahh. Ah, yes. That is so good. That is so very good. Now lick further along. That's it. Caress me with your tongue. That's it! That's it! That is so good!' She adjusted her position so that her buttocks slid further down on the cushions. 'Now,' she cried with her eyes almost closed, 'dip your tongue into my hole. Do it! Do it now!'

Pleasure made her legs thrash so that the boat rocked. It also made her grip him more intently as she pushed him onto her sex then pulled him off again, using his head and his tongue purely for her own sexual gratification.

'But what about him?' she asked herself. What about this tough New York gangster who had swiftly become putty in her hands?

It might have been the softness of her heart that made her think of him, or it might purely have been the heightened pleasure it gave her to order him to pleasure himself. Whatever, she ordered him to take his own penis in his hand.

'Now pull on it till you come,' she demanded. 'But I warn you, do not stop licking me until I come, and only when I climax can you do the same.'

His groan of acquiescence was muffled against the wet slipperiness of her sex.

Virginia opened her eyes a little as he shifted. His head did not leave her lap, but he had adjusted his position so he could more easily get at his penis. A trance-like expression came over his face as he began to pull on it.

Suddenly, he raised his head from her sex, took a deep breath and moaned.

Virginia, tugging his hair so fiercely that it was a wonder it didn't come out of his head, slammed his head back down again.

'I didn't give you permission to stop!' she exclaimed. 'Eat my pussy like I told you to do!'

The first tremor of climax came into being at that very moment when Virginia slammed his head back into her lap. She felt it burst from her as though some great internal quake had cracked itself into existence.

With each lick, probe and tap of the gangster's tongue, her climax became more intense, more piquant. It was like being on the edge of a glassy lake before diving in, and once it had happened and the tremors of climax were washing over her, it was like ripples spreading out over the surface of the water.

She sighed with satisfaction as the last tremors washed over her. Once they had passed, she opened her eyes and looked down on the top of Al's head. With a quick, almost violent jerk, she tugged him from her lap.

He groaned as she came close to him, her mouth just an inch or two from his ear. She saw the blissful confusion in his eyes and the wetness of her sex around his mouth.

'You've done well,' she told him. 'I think you deserve some pleasure yourself.'

She looked down at his penis and the sight of it almost made her come again. It was red as if angry, and its end was slippery with the first beginnings of his come. He closed his eyes and a gasp of exasperated breath rushed from his mouth.

A warning bell sounded inside Virginia's head. Al was entering his own world, his own pleasure, which meant that she was losing control.

She put her hand over his in order to halt his continuing tempo.

'Not in here, stupid boy,' she growled. 'Move nearer the edge and stick it out through the curtains.'

To her great surprise, he did exactly as asked. There he was, kneeling on the cushions, penis in hand and its tip peering out between the curtains. The thought of what it looked like from outside reawakened her earlier excitement.

'Start pulling.' As she said it, she cupped his balls in one hand and scratched at his backside with the other. Just as she had guessed, his backside was nearly as hairy as his pubic region.

'Imagine what anyone outside is seeing,' she said to him with a mocking laugh. 'Imagine how your semen will look swimming around on the canal like a piece of cast-off jellyfish.'

Al Hutchinson, the scourge of the Bronx and a capo with a hundred men in awe of him, groaned in delight. At the sound of her voice, his balls drew up towards his body and semen pulsed from his member and spurted out into the canal.

Chapter 19

Heinrich Zweizer wished he had visited Venice on a business trip previous to this particular visit. At least then he would have known of a house similar to the one in Milan. As it was, both he and Davis Sedglingham, his new-found acquaint-ance – friend would be too familiar a word – would not be in the position they were in now.

In all good faith, both had followed the languid yet dramatic figure of Lawford Parkinson without once thinking that he might take advantge of the excitement that had obliterated their common sense. Like the rats in Hamlin they followed the Pied Piper because visions of Paradise were imagined in their head. And like the rats they had now come face to face with reality.

Parkinson led them across and down two or three canals and into darker tributaries that stank of rotting cabbage and other things too disgusting to mention. Eventually they had disembarked at a pink-washed house whose windows were shuttered against the world outside as if it were keeping itself to itself.

Full of the excitement brought on by contemplating what soft flesh and willing limbs they would encounter, both had followed the tall man in white into the building. Not once did it occur to them to show caution, to ask for a reference, to tell someone else where they were going – just for safety's sake.

Once inside, Davis had wrinkled his nose and remarked on the smell. Zweizer laughed nervously and said it wasn't quite what he had expected either.

The place seemed to be one of darkness and shadows, but not because there wasn't any light. There was. Of a sort. Two flaming torches fell forward at angles. The walls were of the darkest purple, the floors of the blackest marble. There seemed to be no ceiling above them, only darkness.

'Unusual,' Davis muttered. That one word echoed around them. Ultimately, it had been joined by the hollowness of footsteps; three, perhaps four people. Lawford seemed to fade into the shadows.

Zweizer cried out and Davis had struggled as they were pounced upon, stripped of valuables and each bent double over some trestle-like contraption to which both their ankles and wrists were then tightly bound.

'What are you going to do with us?' asked David Sedglingham, tightening his buttocks as he thought of the worst possible thing that could happen.

He heard laughter and was thankful that it was feminine. A woman's feet, clad in plain black shoes, came into view. The feet in those shoes were slightly swollen and so were the ankles above them. Unsympathetic hands gripped hold of his hair and jerked his head upwards. The face that looked into his sent shivers down his spine.

Her eyes were as black as coal. So were her eyebrows which furrowed into a deep vee over the bridge of her nose. Huge breasts, unfettered by any undergarment, strained against the coarse, black material of her dress.

She grinned. If she had sixteen teeth in her head, he conceded her lucky. Suddenly she thrust her huge breasts forward so that his head was between them, his senses assailed by their sponginess and the aura of stale sweat that emanated from the valley between. Davis gagged on the feel and the smell of it. He did his best to hold his breath, then gasped as she released him. She laughed again.

She spoke in Italian. Her tone of voice was enough to tell Sedglingham that she meant them only harm. He looked to Zweizer for translation.

170

'What does she want?' he cried. He was fearful of the answer. 'Zweizer,' he repeated in a voice approaching panic, 'what the bloody hell does she want?'

'Money.' Zweizer's voice trembled.

'I thought so. Haven't they taken enough? They've got everything. Including our clothes! Dirty bitch!'

Although not understanding his language, the woman obviously understood his tone. She grabbed a handful of his hair with one hand and slapped his face with the other. She shook him like a dog does a rat before letting his head go. Her attention went to Zweizer. Davis could hear him groaning, but couldn't see what the woman was doing to him. Whatever it was, she was doing it from behind.

The woman was again extolling whatever she wanted in rushed and slightly coarse Italian.

'What the devil is it, Zweizer?'

He heard the sound of slapping on bare flesh. Each slap was followed by a sharp cry from Zweizer.

'What's she doing?' he asked.

'She's smacking me,' wailed Zweizer.

Davis did not ask where she was smacking him. The reverberation of the slaps denoted the area was a fleshy one so it had to be his backside.

Davis closed his eyes and shook his head with exasperation. He flexed his arms against his bonds and wished he could get hold of the crone's neck – before she subjected him to the same humiliation Zweizer was at present enduring.

'Tell her we're gentlemen,' he said suddenly as the beads of sweat that had been on his brow ran down into his eyes. 'Tell her she can have whatever she wants. We have money. Is that what she wants?'

'Yes. Money,' Zweizer wailed as more slaps sounded. 'She wants more money.' An almighty hiss sounded, as though a riding whip had just swished through the air. Zweizer let out a loud yell. Davis stiffened against his

171

bonds, his whole body almost at one with the wooden trestle he was bound to.

'Then get her some. Get her some!'

Whether the woman had detected some semblance of weakness in him, Davis didn't know. He only winced as the first slap landed on his buttocks. In response, he clenched them together and groaned. Then he cried out as her fingers, thick as sausages, encircled his scrotum and gathered his fruit into the palm of her hand.

She cackled like a witch recently escaped from Macbeth or, more likely, from some Italian lunatic asylum. The cackle continued through her words. Zweizer interpreted.

'She says one of us is to go and get more money. If not they will take compromising photographs of us and take them to the train.'

'Then let them,' Davis sneered. 'If they want to show us naked, so what?'

'With men,' Zweizer added forlornly.

Davis gulped. His worst nightmare had come true. This was the reason they were naked and bending over these trestles. In response to the picture in his mind, he gripped his buttocks together that much more tightly. The old woman's cackle increased in menace. He shivered with horror at the touch of her rough palms as she caressed each firm flank. Her hands dropped to grasp his haunches tightly. There was no doubt as to his fate as she began to jerk her fat abdomen against his backside in a gross parody of what could well happen to him if she didn't get paid.

His flesh burned then was cooled as a draft of air entered. Somewhere, a door had opened.

Davis tried to look over his shoulder. Something seemed to scrape across the floor.

The woman spoke again.

'I have told them I am a banker. They say it is I who must go and get some money.' Zweizer sobbed before finding his voice. 'They've brought in a camera.'

172

A tripod. Davis balked at the thought of it. Not just the shame of the photographs, though that was bad enough. But the thought of having his rear invaded by some Italian stallion was too much to bear. He struggled so much that the trestle he was mounted on jerked away from the ground. His action brought swift retribution. The whip he had heard course through the air and land on Zweizer's backside now landed on his.

'Get them some money,' he growled blackly. 'Get them some money!'

'They say they will keep you here till I bring it back.'

'Then do it. Fast!'

Davis heard Zweizer yelp. The flash of a photograph being taken followed. Male voices interspersed with that of the woman. Zweizer went on groaning in time with whatever was happening to him. Davis tried to close his mind to it. The best he could do was to close his eyes and hope it would all be over for Zweizer shortly. He hoped more avidly that the same fate would pass him by.

A man cried out in ecstasy at the same time as Zweizer cried out in shame. Davis squeezed his eyes shut until the sound of ecstasy had finished and the sound of shame had diminished. Although he was covered in sweat, he shivered at what might be in store.

The woman addressed Zweizer.

'What did she say?' cried Davis, his voice trembling.

'She says she will keep the plates of this photograph until I get back from the bank. If I don't . . .'

'And me?' The voice of Lord David Sedglingham quivered like reeds in a north wind.

'They'll do the same to you if I don't get back in time.'

The legs of the wooden trestle scraped and tapped on the floor as Davis was overcome by sheer terror.

'Get it, Zweizer! Get that money now!'

Whilst his master was out seeking sexual gratification at a

Venetian brothel, Mario was stuffing what little he owned into the same battered case he had used when first leaving home.

With hopeful heart he pulled on his jacket then slicked back the thick thatch of dark hair from off his tan brow.

Even as he checked his appearance in the mirror, a knock came to the door. He turned and looked at it with absolute adoration as if he could see through it, as if it were her sultry looks and slender body he could see there. Radiant with happiness, he took a deep breath before asking her to come in. He knew it was her, knew she would look just as glowing as the image he carried in his mind.

'Are you ready?' Her face, just as he had supposed, was bright with excitement. Cheeks were flushed, lips were red and deep dimples accompanied her smile.

She was dressed in a bright red dress with matching navy and red hat and shoes. A beige and tan suitcase sat on the floor either side of her. Her perfume wafted through the doorway and, as it did so, the smell of masculinity and of Davis Sedglingham was instantly overcome.

Mario just stared until he could find his tongue. 'You look lovely,' he said at last.

A sudden thought came to him. He looked briefly around the cabin behind him. Petula's smile lessened.

'He's not still here is he?' she whispered. Her eyes widened and looked around the cabin as if she expected Davis Sedglingham to jump out at any minute.

Despite the fact that his arm ached from the most recent beating he had received from his master, Mario stretched it out bravely and pulled her to him.

'No,' he said softly, shaking his head, his eyes bright with need. 'No. He is not here. I saw some friends of mine in Venice – my niece – my sister's daughter. Her father is American. I arranged with him that they will be distracted long enough for us to make our escape. Long enough for us to make love too.'

'Come in,' he said, and his face became like the sun as it broke into a happy smile. 'I think we will leave my master with one more embarrassment before we go.'

Puzzlement on her face, Petula let Mario take charge and pull both her and her cases inside the door. Where her cases went, she followed. Mario closed and bolted the door behind her before taking her in his arms.

In the midst of an embrace, their lips met and all the abuse they had both endured from two different men melted in the heat of it. They clung together, breast against breast, hardening male penis against moistening female genitals. Thigh rubbed longingly against thigh and it was a while before Mario managed to speak.

'We will now take advantage of his bed, seeing as he has so often taken advantage of my good nature.'

Petula, who had been brought up in Hell's Kitchen and had thought herself lucky to land a man like Al Hutchinson, now knew she had not been lucky, just fated.

The love Al had shown her was based on owning, controlling. Emotion had been measured by what she was prepared to do and endure in exchange for a fur coat, a silver bracelet, or a cocktail dress costing more than five hundred bucks. Now she knew that what she had shared with Al had not been love but need. Her need was to survive, his was to control. Their only common ground had been the circumstances of their birth and the sex they shared, sex which was based on brutal advance on his part and instant submission on hers.

Love with Mario was a different kettle of fish. Both had been born into poverty and both had been abused in exchange for surviving.

Petula felt no puzzlement at what Mario had said or what he was doing. His darkness, his broad shoulders and muscular body completely subjugated any questions she might have wanted to ask him. Petula was unmistakably and utterly in love with him.

175

It was this love and this trust in him that let him lead her into Davis Sedglingham's bedroom, the most luxurious on the train.

Pale green panels with mother-of-pearl inlay encompassed the small but beautifully appointed room. A thick counterpane in a mix of gold thread and the same pale green as the walls covered the bed.

Petula barely noticed the sumptuousness of her surroundings. She needed no prompting to take her clothes off. Her eyes held a strange, wild hunger when she at last regarded the bronzed body of her darling lover.

Once he had kissed and fondled her breasts, he told her to lie down on the bed.

Eyes shining with adoration, Petula did exactly as he asked, her body sliding onto the silky sheets as though grateful for their cool, delicate caress.

For a moment Mario stood at the foot of the bed, a look of wonder on his face. He feasted his eyes on the pertness of her breasts, the generous proprotions of her nipples. Like a man who has been blind and at last can see, he let his gaze follow the golden hair that formed a wildly luxuriant coxcomb and ran from between her thighs and up over the plumpness of her pubic mound.

Eyes full of love, Petula watched as Mario went to his master's dressing table and took hold of a particularly beautiful bottle. It was of blue glass and had a gold top to it.

Hypnotised both by the bottle and Mario's slow, sensual movements, Petula's gaze followed his movements as the bottle was undone. A perfume, unseen but provocatively sweet to the nostrils, seeped and spread upon the air.

With slow deliberation, Mario poured some of the sweet-smelling liquid onto his palms. He smiled at her.

'Do not be afraid,' he said. 'It is only oil. See? I am using it purely for your comfort. Everything must be smooth. Everything must be like silk or satin.'

176

Fascinated, Petula watched as Mario rubbed his palms together. Calmly and with the greatest of concentration, he took his penis in one hand and covered it in a generous sheen of oil. He did the same with his other hand, yet left enough to smooth over her sex so that her hairs lay flat against her flesh. With that same hand and the residue of oil, he anointed her labia and ran more of the slick through her legs and upwards into her vagina.

Petula groaned and lifted her buttocks off of the bed. His fingers worked through her sex and into her body. Yet all the time as she enjoyed his ministrations, her eyes never left the sight of his penis which pulsed with hardness and glistened with oil.

Lost in desire, Petula saw him as though through a swirling mist. He knelt between her legs then leaned forward so that the outside of his thighs rubbed against the inside of hers. He kissed her before placing his hands on either side of her shoulders. His muscles rippled as he braced his arms. Their eyes met and their breathing seemed suspended in the air between them. At last, with one small excited sigh, he pushed himself into her.

So gentle was his intrusion, so smooth the course, that Petula barely had a chance to fully appreciate it until his pubic bone was tight against hers.

Trickles of the sweet-smelling oil mixed with her sexual juices and seeped out around his shaft. Delicately, like nectar from a flower, it licked in slow rivulets between her outer and inner lips and trickled less cautiously between the cheeks of her behind and onto the sheets.

It occurred to her that Lord Sedglingham's bed was being stained and, although Mario had not explained this was his intention, she had no need to question him about it. She already knew the answer and had followed the same sort of reasoning herself. Back in the bed she had shared with Al Hutchinson, she had left a mass of coloured silk all piled up in pretty little heaps. They had once been his favourite ties;

garish things of the brightest colours and the most satin of sheens. Now they were no more than little bits of nothing. Just like her and Al.

She and Mario were everything; two halves of the same whole. Mario's orgasm rose in time with hers. Soaring into the sky. Higher and higher they climbed until reaching the highest point of all, then fell like a single feather from sky to earth.

Chapter 20

Alphonse, in his guise as Dorothy Plumber, got back to the train before either Virginia or Raymonde. Before climbing aboard, he had to stand back as a dark-haired man and a brash blonde both carrying suitcases climbed quickly down.

They giggled and barely glanced at him before they raced away from the train. Alphonse blinked as he watched them go. The girl had been nearest to him, her buttocks hard against his groin. Alphonse sniffed a hint of perfume she had left in her wake. In response, his cock thrust forward from between his legs. Oddly enough, he was glad that he was wearing a skirt rather than trousers.

Unlike Raymonde, Alphonse was quite enjoying his disguise. There was something uniquely naughty about wearing no knickers beneath his clothing. Perhaps it was something to do with the fact that he was a man dressed as a woman and no one else knew that. It was also because the cool air felt good as it circulated like soft fingers over his balls and caressed his cock like the lips of an unseen lover.

A sudden movement caught his eye. The crowd near the arched entrance to the station were moving aside like corn bending before a sudden breeze. The greyish green of uniforms and the feathered plume of an officer's hat bobbed through the dividing crowd. Alphonse did not linger. All the same, he did check the quickness of his movements. After all, his current disguise was a better defence than any masculine speed.

But his mind was still working more quickly than his

body. In his haste he fled one carriage too many and burst into the wrong cabin.

Agnetha Zweizer, sponging herself between her legs and clad in nothing but her stockings and garters, opened her mouth to shriek but stopped when she saw who it was.

'Miss Plumber. What are you doing in here?'

Alphonse tried hard to avert his eyes from the lean, white body.

With a hint of desperation, he glanced nervously back at the door. Already he could hear the sound of boots marching up and down the corridor. He knew very well that the soldiers were searching for him.

It was difficult but he managed to pull himself together. 'I am so sorry. I am in the wrong cabin I think.' Clutching his handbag, his eyes dropped to the golden curls that curved in a delicate arc up towards her belly. A blush came to his cheeks.

Agnetha saw the blush but gave no sign herself of being embarrassed. She glanced down to where he was looking and a small tingle of residual pleasure rippled through her body. Hans had kissed and licked her to distraction, and now having this awkward-looking woman staring at her little treasure was making her hot again. Putting down the sponge with which she was cleansing away the stickiness of orgasm, she stepped towards Dorothy.

'Do you like it?' she asked, her eyes shining as old memories of schooldays and adoring school friends came back to her mind.

Swallowing and feeling suddenly as though he were twice the size he was, with eight arms and six legs, Alphonse merely nodded. Would she see the way his penis was poking into his skirt, he asked himself? Would she see the gob of juice that had transferred itself to the dull, grey silk?

It seemed not. Agnetha's eyes did not drop below his chin. He could see a gleam in them and wondered why she did not cover her nakedness. His heart thudded against his ribs as her white, cool body came close. Her round breasts were within his reach, her nipples pointing at him as though begging him to touch, and her sex . . . Oh, her sex and those golden hairs just waiting for his fingers to run through them, his tongue to slick them wetly to her flesh, his lips to suck them into his mouth . . .

Agnetha laughed so suddenly it made him start. 'Do not look so worried, my dear. You secret is safe with me.'

Still smiling, she tapped her finger on one of his breasts. She did not appear to notice that they were different from those of any other women.

'Secret?' It was all he could say. His mouth was too dry to say anything else. He fiddled with his handbag and held it tightly in his white-gloved hands.

'Of course,' said the smiling Agnetha. 'I can see we have similar tastes. It is what comes of spending your youth only with women.'

Alphonse wished he'd been that lucky, but was too dumbstruck to comment. He clutched his handbag more tightly as Agnetha's fingers began to fondle his.

All trace of coldness left her face. Suddenly, she was like a child again, a schoolgirl pleading, wheedling for what she wanted. 'Please,' she said in a small, almost silly voice. 'Please lick my pussy.'

The fingers that had so tightly clutched the handbag were now easily prised away. Alphonse was speechless. He stared at her. Had he heard right?

'I am sorry, madame. What was that you said?'

She snuggled closer to him at the same time as flinging his handbag to one side. 'Kiss my lips, then kiss my pussy.'

Alphonse did exactly as ordered. Afraid of her smelling his masculine odour through the violet water he was wearing, his kiss on her lips was short. Besides, he was keen to lower himself to her more verdant fruit, the round, firm breasts, the flat belly and the golden crown of pubic curls.

181

As he moved down towards her most hallowed treasure, he held her at the waist and kissed each of her white breasts. He could have lingered a while longer on her plump areolae and her hard nipples, but he could not afford to do that. This, he had decided, was a woman who liked the attention of other women. He wondered if her husband had ever penetrated her. Surely he had? After all, a marriage has to be consummated. Did the Zweizers have any children?

He didn't know. All he did know was that he would do exactly as she wanted. When it was done he would deal with his own sexual relief in solitude.

'That is so good,' she murmured as he kissed her belly and poked his tongue into her navel. 'And my nipples are so hard I will have to deal with them myself.'

Thank God, thought Alphonse, grateful that she would not be running her fingers through his wig which would have no hope of staying in place under pressure.

Kneeling before her, he took hold of her hips, his eyes full of the golden pubes that were still damp from the sponging she had been giving them.

At first he merely blew on the curling thatch, watched the pinkness of her flesh appear and smelt her femininity. Then, with a sigh that was a mix of pain as well as pleasure, he poked out his tongue so it slid into the very opening of her slit.

She groaned as his tongue progressed, flicking delicately over the small, hard nub that sat like a cherry stone between flesh as silky and delicate as a butterfly's wings.

He imagined what effect it was having on her, the flickerings of sensation starting between the moist folds of flesh and flowing through her body.

Imagining was not a good thing for him – not if he was to maintain his disguise.

He squeezed his eyes tightly shut as the sound of boots paused outside the cabin door.

'Hello! Hello in there!' The harsh voice was accompanied by a sharp rapping on the door.

'Go away. Can you not leave a woman in peace? Go away!'

Agnetha's voice had lost the sweet, youthful tone she had adopted towards 'Dorothy'. Now it was back to its former coldness, its former authority.

'But, madame—' the voice began.

'What do you want, you stupid man?'

'We are searching for a dangerous criminal, madame, and if we could just come in—'

'I am Frau Zweizer. My husband is director of the Zweizer International Bank in Zurich. If I had a criminal in here I would hand him over. As it is there is just me and a female companion. Now go away!'

Alphonse buried his nose in the clutch of golden hair he had so admired. There was a tense moment of silence whilst boots shuffled indecisively just beyond the door. Alphonse closed his eyes that much tighter. 'If I am to die,' he thought to himself, 'let me drown in her juices, suffocate in the odour of a woman.'

The moment passed. Sounds of scuffles mixed with shouted orders as those outside turned away and went rapping on other doors.

Despite the fact that his penis was so tight with suppressed semen that it was almost painful, Alphonse went to his task with greater gusto than before.

In thankful gratitude that she had been so intimidating to those beyond the door, he pushed his tongue into her vagina, his nose kissing her clitoris as though he were some Eskimo greeting a friend. Then, as her hips began to jerk against his face, he sucked in the juices of her orgasm and groaned as if the pleasure she felt really belonged to him.

In the belief that he had the same between his legs as she did, Agnetha offered to give him the same service. He was wise enough to decline. Much as he would have liked to see her shocked surprise when his penis came into view, he knew the soldiers were not too far away and his disguise was his only defence. So he declined her offer and was glad to see the relief on her face. Obviously Agnetha preferred to have it done to her rather than do it to anyone else.

'Do come again,' she said as she handed him his handbag.

Alphonse nodded. Their hands touched. Agnetha smiled as she regarded the white gloves he wore.

'I liked feeling your gloves on my body. It added a certain something; like adding seasoning to dinner.'

The military had left the train by the time he left her. Once in the confines of the cabin, Alphonse kicked off the same shoes that Raymonde had complained of and followed that with having a good scratch at his groin. His penis reminded him that it was still there by raising itself and forming a pyramid in the grey silk skirt he was wearing.

He fixed a thoughtful look on the bulge that was rapidly forming in the skirt. His breathing came a little faster, a little more intensely. As though having made a sudden decision, he lifted the shiny, slippery fabric and, with a mix of pride and curiosity, watched as the gleaming head of his weapon rose majestically into view.

He thought of Agnetha's pubic hair; the feel of it, the smell of it. He smiled at his penis, then with only one finger at first, he tapped at its shiny head. One pearl drop of fluid stood trembling on the crown of his shaft. Delicately, so as not to disturb it, he tapped at the silky moistness. Once most of it was transfered to his fingertip, he rubbed it all over the crown of his stem so it gleamed as if it had been touched with silver. Round, purple and shining with fluid, it now stood proudly upright.

Alphonse regarded it sagely, though it was excitement he was feeling. Each lewd thought that ran through his mind made his penis pulse slightly as though it too were imagining where it might go in such a stiff situation. What would it have been like, he wondered, to push it into Frau Zweizer's hidden portal? But he knew it was not possible. Frau Zweizer would not contemplate such a thing. She was a woman who liked her pussy being eaten and not fucked.

Instantly, he thought of someone else whose body was better than the Swiss woman's and whose appetite for sex knew no bounds.

Thinking of Virginia at the same time as playing with himself made his prick harder; made it dance that much more. He closed his eyes and threw back his head. His flesh was hot and hard in his hand.

In his mind he pretended it was Virginia doing this to him. In reality he was getting close to a climax. As he got nearer he had to open his eyes and search for a suitable receptacle in which to secrete his semen. His gaze raced over his surroundings.

Just when he thought that his searching was in vain the door opened. He gasped, but continued what he was doing. What had been only in his mind now stood before him in the flesh. Virginia was staring at him, mouth hanging open. The object of his sexual fantasy was standing before him and her presence further ignited his rising excitement.

Virginia took a very deep breath before closing the door behind her. Her eyes did not leave his penis and her red lips remained parted. The tip of her tongue flicked out from between her teeth and wetted her bottom lip.

The moment seemed suspended between them. Both were getting something they wanted from this, yet soon, someone had to say something. It was Virginia who broke the silence.

'I take it something has excited you.' Her voice was low and husky. Her breasts rose and fell in rapid succession – as though she were having trouble breathing.

Alphonse groaned, took a deep breath, but still continued to pull himself off. He managed to nod and mutter a muffled 'yes'.

Virginia took the few steps from the door to where he lay sprawled in the chair. 'Let me help you.' Her voice was full of intent but also possessed a certain kind of excitement that was born of the thrill of having found him like this. Her face was flushed and her eyes glittered with instant desire.

Without another word, she knelt between his legs.

Alphonse groaned as, wide-eyed, she eased his penis from his hands and took it into hers. He saw her dark lashes swoop over her cheeks as she bent her head and took his erection into her mouth. He groaned as the feel of her hands on his shaft sent shivers through his flesh. He sank backwards as her mouth went up and down his stem, her tongue licking around the crown and poking deftly into its single opening.

Virginia felt his penis shudder on her tongue and tasted the saltiness of the first droplets of secretion. One set of fingers wrapped around his stem whilst her other hand cupped his balls.

Her tongue worked with amazing and mind-blowing dexterity. The penis of the ecstatic Alphonse pulsated with delight with each suck of her mouth and the ministrations of her tongue.

Ever since he had joined them, Virginia had wanted to do this. Rich men might be her aim, but virile young men were most definitely her pleasure.

She caressed his bare thighs and inhaled the scent of his pubic hair which intermittently tickled the end of her nose.

She sucked at him hungrily, almost as if it were some solace after allowing Al Hutchinson's seed to spill into the waters of the canal.

Such was the sensitivity of her tongue, that it was not too long before she felt the throbbing of the vein that ran up the back of his penis. Suddenly, his shaft tightened and thickened. From experience, she knew it was almost ready to carry its load to its tip and thence to her tongue.

Higher and higher it climbed. More and more throbbed the virile weapon within the moist confines of her mouth. At last, with a sharp jerk of his hips and a pulsating pumping of his stem, his seed gushed out and hit the back of her throat before trickling in a salty mass down into her body.

So intently did she concentrate on receiving all that

Alphonse had to offer, that she took little notice of the knocking on the door and the muffled announcement that there was a message for her. By the time her senses had returned to something nearing normality, the fact that a messenger had knocked was forgotten. Therefore she did not notice he had pushed the envelope under the door a little too roughly. It ended up lying under a chair and next to the wastepaper basket.

But by then, Raymonde had also returned to stand inside the door, watching until she had swallowed the last of the Italian's semen.

Like the message, Virginia gave little sign that he had been noticed. But she knew he was there and his presence gave greater impetus to her actions and also greatly heightened her enjoyment.

Raymonde hardly wanted to admit to himself that he was enjoying being a spectator or that an erection was stirring below his waist. It seemed so sordid somehow and, yet, he had been mesmerised by the sight of her head bobbing up and down on the Italian fugitive's penis.

'I could grow accustomed to this,' he told himself. 'I could really learn to live with this, to have the woman I love being fucked by another man.'

Although he felt no guilt about his admission, he put the thought away and told himself to stop. But he couldn't tear his eyes away from what was happening, and he couldn't get the thought out of his mind that this was the most arousing thing he had ever experienced.

Chapter 21

They left Venice that evening for the short run to Trieste, a city divided into pieces by diplomats and differing cultures.

Davis Sedglingham said surprisingly little about Mario running off with the American gangster's girlfriend. Once Venice was behind them, there was a singular attitude about him, a seeking out of quiet corners and a solitary seating arrangement at meal times.

Still piqued at his treatment of her and relishing the chance to undermine his arrogant self-confidence, Virginia looked diligently for the opportunity to mention it.

Finally, when dinner was long over, the clock was ticking towards midnight and only a handful of passengers were left sipping cocktails in the bar and comparing details of their experiences in Venice, Virginia finally cornered him.

As per his current custom, he was sitting in a quiet corner. He did not acknowledge her presence though her shadow fell over him.

'Mister Sedglingham,' she purred, barely able to disguise the rancour in her voice. 'I hear Venice took up so much of your time that an elopement occurred in your absence. What interesting things you must have got up to that you failed to get back in time to stop your servant running away with the American woman.'

She let the end of her cigarette holder run in an obviously provocative manner along her bottom lip as she smiled.

Davis Sedglingham slammed shut the book he was reading and snorted a rushed breath down his nose before looking up at her. He attempted a smile but it was so strained it ended up as a grimace. 'Venice was as fine a European city as any I've visited. There were lots of things to see there.'

Smoke from her cigarette curled like a soft blue veil between them. Virginia fancied she saw a hint of embarrassment on Davis's face. The laugh that followed was loud but nervous. 'I cannot watch over my responsibilities all the time.'

Virginia arched her eyebrows. 'Oh! Is that what your valet was? A responsibility?'

Davis glared. 'Of course. He was a servant. That's all. Just a servant.'

Inwardly, Virginia called herself a fool. She had been on the verge of inviting him back to her cabin and thus into her bed. Once he had said what he had said, her mind went back to the days when she had been nothing but a servant, getting up at dawn to light the fire, lay the breakfast table and help a selfish, foolish woman get dressed. Suddenly she was glad that Davis Sedglingham had brushed her aside. Although she wished for a lover who could provide her with the lifestyle of a lady as well as fulfill all her sexual needs, she came to an instant conclusion. No matter his riches, looks or sexual attraction, she also wished for a man with a heart. Davis Sedglingham's heart, she decided, had turned to stone long ago.

But she had no intention of leaving him without firing some last-minute barb. The retort was laden with the sweetest of smiles. 'A servant, but well endowed so I hear. Funny isn't it, Davis darling, that no matter how much money a man might have, it doesn't necessarily follow that his shaft matches his wealth. Tell me, which is the smaller of yours, your bank account or your cock?'

He glared. Her barb had hit home. She smiled and, without waiting for any response, turned on her heel. Seething and annoyed that she could have set her cap at such a shallow man, she walked back to where Alphonse was waiting for her, looking decidedly drunk and not at all ladylike.

When she glanced back to where Davis had been sitting, his seat was empty. She caught a brief glimpse of the back of one leg as he exited the cocktail carriage. For the first time in a long while, Virginia felt lonely and this made her think of Emerson Whitman, her rich but distant Australian lover. Where was he now, she mused. Thinking of him made her want to see him again.

But she couldn't. This was now and she was travelling down to Istanbul on the Orient Express. Emerson, covered in sweat and reeking of hard muscles and hard labour, was probably riding around his many acres and counting how much wool and mutton he was likely to produce during the next year. Her imaginings were interrupted by her travelling companion.

Alphonse, a glittering brightness in his eyes and a pinkness on his cheeks, squeezed her thigh once she had settled herself.

'Don't do that,' she snapped. 'You're supposed to be a woman, remember?'

A stupid smile spread over the Italian's face and, when it did, his good looks retreated. Alphonse had been drinking too much for a man and far too much for the sort of woman he was pretending to be.

'Do not worry yourself about that pig, madam. What need do you have of this man when you have me?'

Virginia looked nervously around her. Alphonse was being loud and getting louder. Luckily the bar was empty except for the barman. She made an instant decision.

'I think we should go to bed, Dorothy darling.'

Her smile was bright and indicated to Alphonse that going to bed might mean a lot more than going to sleep, although she had no intention of cuddling up to a drunken Italian.

191

'Ah yes,' he hissed through his silly grin. 'We will go to bed, Virginia. Just you and I. You and me. Virginia and Al . . .'

Virginia quickly clamped a hand over his mouth.

'Come along, Dorothy. Quieten down or you won't get to sleep, will you?'

'I don't want to . . .'

Virginia lugged Alphonse to his feet. He tottered on the unsteady heels, knees splaying outwards as he lolled briefly against her.

Luckily the barman had his back to them, but for a moment, Virginia was wondering whether she'd have to ask him for help in getting 'Dorothy' off to bed.

Luck came in the form of Raymonde who had obviously put his American widow to bed and had made sure she had received a vigorous enough nightcap – a sexual one rather than a liquid one – to make her sleep soundly till morning.

'I'm afraid my friend's had too much to drink,' she explained to Raymonde with a weak grin.

Her heart seemed to leap as she looked into his eyes. She saw something there, some kind of gratefulness that she really did need him. He probably saw the jealousy in hers. Why did he have to suck up to that American woman?

As he got on 'Dorothy's' other side, it occurred to Virginia for the first time that Raymonde was doing no more or less than she had intended. She had specifically booked on this train in order to find herself a rich lover. So far she had not had a lot of success. But he had and that's what rankled.

At that moment, the barman offered his services.

'No,' said Virginia quickly. 'It's alright. We can manage.'

'You're depriving that man of his tip,' Raymonde said once the barman had gone.

'Then I've saved money,' she muttered as they eased a half-dozing Alphonse out of the bar carriage.

'You'll have to pay me instead.' Raymonde's eyes met hers in such a way as to make his meaning clear. She instantly knew he would want some reward for his assistance. Such knowledge made her want to run Alphonse along the corridor that led to her quarters. But his legs were sagging and one of his false breasts was nestling at his waist.

Once safe from prying eyes, they undressed Alphonse and tumbled him onto his bed. Just so that the cabin steward would not drop the early morning tea in shock, they dressed him in a long pink nightgown, pulled the bed-clothes up over his chin, and made sure his face, which was already showing signs of stubble regrowth, was turned to face the wall.

Breathless with the exertion of it all, Virginia wiped at her forehead and leaned against the wall. Her eyes followed Raymonde's actions as he turned to face her.

My, but his eyes were so alluring and his body was so virile. A wisp of dark hair curled down over his brow and she had an instant urge to touch it and push it up back where it belonged.

She reached out. Raymonde, whose eyes were looking with longing into hers, caught hold of her wrist before she could carry out what she had an urge to do.

'How dare you!' she exclaimed, pulling away from him. 'Let go of my wrist. You're hurting me.'

Raymonde did not move. Virginia knew from the expression in his eyes that he did not believe what she was saying. She hardly did herself, but it was damned difficult to accept that she wanted to have sex with this tough, good-looking Canadian when such a short while ago he had been having sex with his American woman.

But he was hard to resist. Hard work had formed his whole body to make it exactly the way she liked it. His shoulders had been broadened, so he had told her, by swinging axes against tall maple and redwoods back in the forests of Alberta. And, like a tree, she was falling too.

He said nothing to her, just drew her body closer to his. At first she resisted, mouthing a sudden no. But her body would not resist him. Neither could her mind control the sensations that were pouring like treacle all over her skin.

The firmness of her breasts met the hardness of his chest before he bent his head and covered her lips with his.

At first she kept her mouth tightly shut so that his tongue could not dip between her teeth, but to do so became impossible.

Her body was telling her to give in. Her mind was telling her she could not possibly hold out. Submission was inevitable and something about that made her slightly angry.

Anger was short-lived. So was the rigid stance. Once in his arms and feeling the heat of his body and the moist warmth of his breath on her face and her neck, she was lost and could do nothing except submit.

Just as she thought her knees were going to buckle under her and she wanted to be loved forever by this man, he stopped kissing her and spoke quietly but very firmly.

'I was going to take you into my cabin, but I think we will stay here. Take off your clothes.'

She glanced swiftly at the sleeping Alphonse before complying. It was as if her hands were not hers but had been borrowed by Raymonde.

All the time she was removing her clothes, Virginia's gaze stayed fixed on her lover. Not once did he offer to help her undress. After lighting a cigarette, he leaned languidly against the door, his eyes piercing her flesh as each item of clothing was removed.

'Now turn round,' he said once she was completely naked. 'I want to look at you from the back.'

Virginia could not have known it, but Raymonde was almost dizzy with expectation. And yet he knew inherently that he must proceed in this manner. He had perceived something in Virginia that she had not perceived in herself. Every so often she required someone else to be in control.

That was what she would want in a lover – or even, thought Raymonde, two lovers. Imagining her with two men at the same time made his senses reel with desire. It took a great deal of effort to find his voice.

'Walk over to the window.' He said it casually yet not without demand.

Virginia paused and for a moment she thought of rebellion. But as she looked at the firm set of his jaw and the unflinching stare of his eyes, it came upon her that she wanted to obey him.

Trembling slightly, she went over to the window.

'Pull the curtains back,' he ordered.

Wide-eyed, Virginia glanced at him over her shoulder, her lips parted as though she wanted to protest. But no words came. Raising her arms, she slipped her hands between the curtains and pulled them back.

In the window she saw her breasts, her belly and her curving hips reflected darkly, the room behind her more brightly.

'Stretch your arms above you,' he ordered. 'Hold onto the curtain track.'

Again, as the night-time world sped by, she did as he ordered. The coldness of the glass was delicious against her breasts.

Would any eyes, she wondered, be looking up at the well-lit train as it sped past? Would they see her nakedness? Would they wonder, as she was wondering, what would happen next?

Uncaring about such things, she purred with pleasure as his hands came around her ribs until her breasts were covered by his palms, gripped by his fingers.

Senses reeling, she gasped and closed her eyes as the tip of his penis divided her buttocks then slid slowly downwards until it was nudging at her vagina.

His lips came close to her ears. His breath was warm as he spoke of what he was going to do to her, of how he wished

195

there were eyes out there beyond that window, watching as she yielded to him, as both experienced pleasure.

His hands ran down over her hips, her thighs and down her legs. He kissed each buttock in turn, then, as he slid a chair each side of her, he bid her place one knee on each of them.

'I want him to do all of this,' she thought to herself, aware that the most sensitive parts of her sex were throbbing and heavy with anticipation.

She did as he requested, one knee on each chair so her legs were further parted and her bottom stuck out lewdly yet unashamedly behind her

She spread her arms out to either side of her, her hands resting on the chair backs. Narrowing her eyes, she could still see the speeding world outside. She also saw Raymonde and felt the warmth of his thighs against hers and the touch of his penis as it invaded her body.

'Imagine what a picture you present,' he whispered against her ear. 'Imagine that all the world is watching us perform. Don't you think that a delicious thought?'

Her eyes stared. Her mouth opened and she gasped in time with his thrusts. 'Yes,' she gasped. 'Ye . . . sss!'

As though part of him, she rocked backwards and forwards with his thrusts, her breasts swinging in time.

Greater impetus, more intense sensations seemed to be ignited by the thought that someone might be watching, that they just might be performing for some unseen audience.

She moaned as her climax began – one small pin head of pleasure, which spread like fine, hot wire, pivoting, whirling outwards, gaining in intensity the more it spread over her body.

Chapter 22

At Trieste, Al Hutchinson decided to invite Virginia to take a trip into the city with him. 'This time,' he said to himself, 'I won't allow that little broad to tell me what she wants. I'll be telling her!'

That might very well have happened if Virginia had consented to accompany him. But she didn't. Much as she still had a yen to get herself a rich lover, her dedication to the task was not as intense as it had been. There was also another reason. At Trieste, Alphonse was leaving the train. It was a matter of yards into Austrian territory where he reckoned he had as good a chance of escaping Italian justice as in the Balkans.

Both Virginia and Raymonde decided to accompany him in a car hired by Raymonde's American widow.

'Head for the water,' Alphonse informed the driver. 'It is only a boat trip from there into Dalmatia.'

They headed off in the opposite direction to where most of the transport seemed to be going.

Virginia looked intently out of the window at two men who were standing beside a long black limousine. The chauffeur was uncommonly good-looking and the man with him was short, plump, but very dapper. The latter was handing what looked like a bundle of money to the former. The plump man Virginia recognised as Herr Heinrich Zweizer.

Mrs Thurbird, resplendent as ever in her favourite colour of tangerine mixed with a hint of grey, swept into a better-looking hotel and demanded afternoon tea, preferably of the breakfast variety.

Without noticing that her three companions were exchanging frantic looks, she attended to the ordering, then noticed that Raymonde was not as close behind her as he had been.

'Raymonde,' she called, earrings dangling with as much subdued anger as her voice, 'is it too much to ask that you pull out a chair for a lady?'

She stood expectantly by a gilt-framed chair with dark brocade upholstery.

With a brief glance and an accompanying wink, Raymonde went to her, not only to assist with the chair, but also to inform her that 'Dorothy' and Virginia were off to the powder room.

Mrs Thurbird raised a gold-framed pince-nez to her nose and peered after them. 'Has that woman brought a change of clothes with her?' she asked, her expression obviously critical of the larger than average handbag 'Dorothy' was carrying.

She did not see the quick raising of Raymonde's eyebrows or the amusement on his face before he answered.

'You could be right. I understand she hasn't been feeling quite herself lately. Women's problems perhaps?'

Mrs Thurbird gave him a sharp look over her gold rims. 'Really, Raymonde. Such delicate matters should not be of general knowledge to gentlemen, and they should certainly not be discussed in the presence of refined ladies – such as myself!'

Raymonde apologised but took the rebuff relatively well. As he sat and attentively listened to the American widow prattle on about all she owned, interspersing her tirade with vague hints on how he might avail himself of a portion of it, Raymonde's gaze alternated between her face and the powder-room door.

Eventually, he saw Virginia's head appear. Her azure

eyes gazed swiftly around the hotel lounge and she threw a wink in his direction. It was hard not to respond but, for the sake of secrecy, he managed. Mrs Thurbird had noticed nothing and neither had anyone else. The coast was clear.

Dressed now in masculine clothes that were neither too poor looking nor too expensive, Alphonse appeared from behind the powder-room door.

Without glancing to where Raymonde was watching him, he kissed Virginia on each cheek, then on the lips. For the briefest of moments, he held her then, to the surprise of both Raymonde and Virginia, instead of making good his escape out of the hotel door, he strode purposefully to where Raymonde and Mrs Thurbird were sitting.

'Madame,' he said, reaching for the widow's hand and holding it to his lips.

A slightly naughty look came over the older woman's face and the hint of a blush appeared on her cheeks. 'I might be getting on a bit,' she said in a low voice, 'but I recognise the scent of a man when I smell it.'

Raymonde and Virginia exchanged puzzled glances.

Mrs Thurbird laughed. 'Don't worry,' she said. 'We are over the border and the woman has become a man. No one knows about it except Mister Hutchinson.'

'What?'

Virginia couldn't help exclaiming loudly. 'What's he got to do with it?'

Mrs Thurbird pursed her lips. 'Alphonse here, who was Dorothy, is now Peter Stowslesk, a man of Trieste. Al Hutchinson of New York isn't here solely on holiday. He's also a man of business. He fixed us up with false papers. So,' she said, grabbing hold of the beaming Italian's hand and looking as happy herself, 'let's say we have tea then get back to the train. I dare say we'll have plenty to occupy us between now and Istanbul.'

Al Hutchinson was feeling grumpy. Not only had he been

unsuccessful with his pursuit of Virginia Vernon, he had lost Petula. Okay, so he'd made a few bucks helping that nutty woman from Baltimore, but what were a few dollars in exchange for female company?

It wasn't his style to wander through the streets of a city, but on this occasion he was feeling well and truly brassed off.

Too busy thinking to notice where he was going, he slipped through a few back streets until he had left the Italian quarter behind.

Austrian accents, and another he was none too sure of, came to his ears. In time, he found he had a crowd of kids following him.

He stopped in his tracks, turned round and stared at them. The kids stopped, their eyes huge as those of hungry wolves, their mouths smiling with ill-concealed menace.

'Get lost!' he shouted. 'Get lost before I . . .'

He stopped what he was going to say. What could he say? This wasn't New York. This was somewhere he didn't know. Those people he did know were back in Milan and Venice. They were business colleagues, members of the same family who ruled by the gun just as he did.

What did it matter that they made things bad for the likes of these people? What did it matter that they fed on ignorance, poverty and depravity? It was his living, his world. But not here, said a small voice in his head. Not here.

It was Raymonde and Virginia who found him. They had been strolling hand in hand and had seen a group of children, laughing and kicking at a bundle of blankets that looked to be half submerged in a particularly mucky puddle.

At their approach, the children ran off. Shocked, they got Al to his feet and helped him back to the train. In the seclusion of his cabin, they stripped off his clothes. He opened his eyes and thanked them, his eyes never leaving

Virginia's face as she sponged his bruises which were deepening to purple even around his crotch.

Raymonde watched her from behind as she gently dabbed around Al's loins. He heard the American make small mewing noises that at first he interpreted as moans. Then, as he watched Al's penis raise its glistening head, he realised he was indeed moaning, but with pleasure not pain.

'I think he wants you to kiss him better,' Raymonde said softly.

Virginia stopped what she was doing and turned round to stare at him.

Raymonde said nothing but just jerked his head in the direction of Al's rising erection.

Virginia looked from Raymonde to Al's face. Al was watching her, arms at his side, his body completely relaxed, completely submissive. His eyes seemed to be begging her to do what Raymonde had suggested.

Slowly, as though she were very carefully considering what she was doing, she put the wet cloth back into the enamel bowl.

Gently, she took hold of his penis and saw it twitch as the coolness of her fingers pulled it out to full length.

Then, just as slowly as everything else she had done, she lowered her head, kissed the tip of his penis, then took the whole thing in her mouth.

She heard Al groan and suddenly what she was doing was so important, so arousing that she positioned herself better so that her mouth was directly over him, her bottom stuck high in the air.

Was it chance that made her stick her bottom out like that, or had she done it intentionally? She knew the answer, knew full well that Raymonde would take advantage of the situation.

She did not protest as she felt her skirt being raised over her hips, felt the buttons of her camiknickers being undone, then its silk sliding down over her hips.

As she tasted the first saltiness of Al's prick on her tongue, she felt the head of Raymonde's cock dip into the tightness of her anus and his fingers into her vagina.

With the newest onslaught into her body, she sucked more earnestly on Al's prick and opened her legs that much more so that Raymonde's penis and hands could get into her more easily.

As though each orifice was intent on reaching its climax first, the areas of her body in which each was situated became more active, more demanding on the fingers that were in her vagina, the cock that was in her mouth and the one that was in her rectum.

Three times the usual pleasure seemed to spread over her as her climax came, violently reaching inwards as though to drag the last sensual vibration from her soul.

'This is a climax of sorts,' she thought afterwards. 'It is all that I am getting on this trip, and yet I do not care. What if Davis Sedglingham is ignoring me. What if I have not found myself the lover of means that I intended. It cannot be helped.'

She confided her thoughts to Raymonde.

'But you have me,' he affirmed.

'But you are not rich,' she returned.

'Ah. But we have not yet reached Istanbul.'

Chapter 23

Aristo and Ariel Kostopoles were becoming agitated with each other, and by the time they got to Belgrade the situation had become quite acute.

'I think this wager has gone far enough. I think now is the time for us to bet on who makes a play for the lady.'

Aristo eyed Ariel for a moment before coming to a decision or making a reply. He scratched cautiously at the mole beneath his chin that was the only physical difference between himself and his brother. He wasn't one for bragging, but he was pretty certain that he was that bit more charming than his brother. After all, Ariel's complexion was a little darker and swarthier than his own.

It would have shocked Aristo to know that his brother was thinking exactly the same thing about him. They were twin brothers, but rather than their thoughts always running along parallel lines, they were sometimes blind to their own weaknesses. In that way at least their thoughts were oddly alike.

'Alright,' said Aristo at last. 'It's a deal.'

They shook on it and, as they alighted from the train and prepared to tour the Savva district of Belgrade which overlooked the surrounding area, they both stopped in front of Virginia, doffed their hats and smiled benignly at her.

'I would appreciate you joining me for dinner tonight,' said the first twin who Virginia could not tell apart from his brother.

'And I would appreciate you joining me for dinner too,' the brother added.

Virginia eyed them with interest. Had she dismissed her quest for future security too quickly? Aware that Raymonde was giving her a hard look, that old feeling of wanting something better for herself rose to the surface, and yet it wasn't quite the same as it had been before. It was as though a battle was going on within. One half of her still hankered after the lifestyle and security she had not been brought up to. The other half was besotted with Raymonde; whose looks made being a sex object seem so attractive.

But this was the first time these two had shown any interest in her. As far as getting a rich lover was concerned, this was her last chance.

Eyes sparkling with anticipation, she looked at each of the twins in turn.

'I'd be delighted to have dinner with both of you. If that would be alright.'

The two brothers exchanged a quick look before turning back to her. 'Both at the same time?' asked Aristo.

Virginia smiled and there was a lot of meaning in her smile. 'Both at the same time,' she said provocatively, and both knew exactly what she meant.

Raymonde walked off in a huff, kicking at the ground in front of him and refusing to accompany Virginia for a trip into the heart of the city.

'I'll find my own way,' he snapped.

'I don't believe I'm feeling like this,' he thought angrily. At first he recognised his feelings as jealousy, then, once he was sitting at a pavement cafe, a few sips of strong coffee seemed to make things that much clearer. It wasn't so much jealousy as the fear of losing her. He could stand seeing her making love with another man. In fact, he was quite happy to watch, to always be at hand should she need him. But he recognised that if she did experience success with the two Greeks, his presence would no longer be required.

Just as another cup of the strong, bitter brew had been brought to him, a man in a summer suit accidentally knocked against his table. It hadn't been the man's fault. It was just that he had become sandwiched between the table and a waiter with a large girth who had not noticed him.

'Aw, I'm so sorry, sport. Can I get you another?'

Before waiting for a reply, he had already summoned the waiter who set about cleaning up the spillage and refilling Raymonde's cup.

'Thanks,' said Raymonde. He looked up at the man who was presently taking off a broad-brimmed Panama. His skin had been tanned by a hot sun, though his hair was streaked with shades of yellow and pale gold. He had blue eyes that smiled as much as his mouth.

'You sound like a colonial,' Raymonde said to him.

'Emerson Whitman. Live in Queensland, or at least, that's where I used to live.'

'Raymonde Leman, Quebec, Canada.' He offered his hand and the two men shook warmly. 'Take a seat.'

The Australian thanked him and Raymonde called for more coffee. 'So what are you doing so far from home?'

The Australian, whose muscles seemed to be attempting to bulge out through the sleeves of his jacket, gave a wry grin. He poked a finger into the brim of his hat so it slid back and sat on the back of his head. 'To tell you the truth, I'm trying to find my courage, and all for a woman.'

Raymonde nodded sympathetically. 'Don't they just take some courage?'

The Australian sighed. 'They sure do, but if you got the hots for them, what can you do?'

Raymonde wasn't too sure what he was getting at, but he had a feeling they'd get there in the end.

'Do everything they least expect. Take them unawares. Excite them with the unusual.'

The Australian laughed. 'You sound as though you like the same sort of woman I do and, hell, I certainly like a bit of variety with what I get up to.' He leaned closer. 'Do you know, back in Alexandria, I had three women in my bed at one time. I tell you, it was one hell of an experience. I did everything I wanted to them, and they did everything I wanted them to do to me – without me having to tell them! There! What do you think of that!'

'I would have liked to have been there. What a sight it must have been.'

Emerson Whitman narrowed his eyes and nodded his approval. 'Yep. It certainly was and, you know, what you've just said makes sense. What can be enjoyed by one man can just as well be enjoyed by two. It's good I've got the money to do that sort of thing. Grossed me nearly a million selling my spread. Course the new bloke won't be worrying about the sheep side of the business. He only wanted it for the ore. Bauxite, I think he called it. Still,' he said before swigging more coffee, 'he's got what he wants, and I'll soon be getting what I want.' He laughed, and Raymonde laughed with him.

The Canadian eyed the Australian but gave no hint on his face of the plan that was forming in his mind. This was the man Virginia had told him about and, strangely enough, he quite liked the guy. 'We've a lot in common,' he thought to himself. He considered carefully what to say next.

'Mind you, there's nothing like a woman with an appetite for sex, and if you've got certain – ' he paused – 'fantasies, certain habits, it makes things even better.'

Although he eyed Emerson in a casual manner, he was alert to the fact that he had captured his immediate attention. He took a deep breath before he clasped his hands together on the table in front of him, then winked and gave the Australian a blokey type of smile.

'Would this woman of yours be open to suggestion? I mean, do you think she would be up to – ' he paused for effect ' – entertaining two blokes at the same time?'

For a moment, Emerson's mouth hung open and his eyes stared. Then a smile spread across his face. 'We . . . ll! I reckon, knowing Ginny, she'd be game alright. If there's one thing Ginny is, it's game for a good bout of sex. Adventurous, you could say. Open to suggestions like you said.'

'Ginny?' Raymonde remarked, his eyes sparkling. 'Do you mean Virginia Vernon?'

Emerson stared. 'You know her?'

'I'm travelling on the same train.' He paused, unsure as to whether he should disclose just how close to her he'd been travelling. Not being a dishonest man, he felt bound to tell the truth.

'I think I have to say that Virginia is the woman I'm talking about. The one who has a liking for having more than one man at a time and is quite partial to having an audience.'

With half a mind that the big Australian might just shove one of his fists into his face, Raymonde straightened as he gauged the man's reaction. He also held his hands in his lap, fists clenched in case he needed to defend himself.

Emerson was silent for a moment, but there was nothing to suggest violence in his eyes. Suddenly he laughed, a big, wide-open-space laugh that seemed to reflect the land he had so lately lived in.

Coffee cups rattled and other diners turned fearful faces towards them as Emerson's big hand thudded on the table. 'That's my girl. That's Virginia. Give her an inch and she wants ten!' His laugh attracted as many fearful looks as the thud of his hand. 'What a girl!' he exclaimed.

Raymonde grinned. 'You don't seem particularly jealous.'

Face still wreathed in smiles, Emerson shook his head. 'I know that woman. I know what she wants and what she's capable of. Probably more so than she does herself.' His face became a little more serious as his smile lessened. 'At least, she *was* game for anything. That's why I thought I'd send her a telegram saying I'd see her in Istanbul and give her the best fucking of her life. Asked her to send a message to Alexandria. Let me know if she'd be up for it. Trouble is, I haven't received any reply to either of the messages.' He looked a little dreamy suddenly. 'Perhaps I should go aboard now and tell her face to face.'

'No.' Raymonde said the word quite sharply. Emerson frowned.

'No?' he repeated questioningly.

Raymonde chanced resting his elbows on the table and leaning forward. 'No,' he repeated. 'Let it be a surprise. Will you be going to Istanbul by car?'

Emerson beamed. 'Yep. Rolls-Royce Silver Ghost. Yellow, it is, and I've got my own driver. Used to drive Bugattis on the circuit. Now he's driving for me.'

Aware that Bugattis were motorcars and Emerson's driver was obviously a racing driver, Raymonde hatched a quick plan.

'Right,' he said. 'We've got an overnight stop on the journey. That way you should get to Istanbul before us. And when we do get there, Virginia will get the surprise of her life.'

Although completely unaware of what was in Raymonde's mind, Emerson beamed. 'She will?'

'Oh, yes,' said Raymonde nodding sagely, his eyes twinkling. 'She'll get a big surprise alright.'

Smiling in the way of a simple man who wants to appear more intelligent than he really is, Emerson nodded his head and kept grinning.

At last he had to ask what was in his mind. 'What sort of surprise?'

Raymonde beckoned with a hooked finger. 'Come closer and I'll tell you.'

Raymonde outlined the details of his plan. 'I've been reading the guidebook,' he explained. 'It's easy to find.'

Emerson got out his own and the pages rustled as he excitedly turned its pages. 'Ah. I've got it. I've got it!'

There was a new spring to Raymonde's step as he walked back to the train.

'I'll catch up with you in Istanbul,' Emerson shouted after him and Raymonde waved his hand in response. All the way back to the train, he whistled as he walked, his step lighter than it had been. His only worry was that Virginia might have made some arrangement with Aristo and Ariel, the dark-eyed, dark-haired and very rich Greeks. But, he assured himself, no matter how persuasive the Greeks were, he knew the ace card he now held was higher than theirs could ever possibly be.

Chapter 24

Half hidden in an evening mist that failed in any way to dim the gold dome of Haga Sophia, Istanbul brooded at the side of the calm Bosporous.

Raymonde knew that Virginia had slept with the twin Greeks the night before. Alone, he had listened to the tune of the train as it sped along the silvery rails to the city that spanned Europe and Asia.

In his mind he had imagined her body, soft with a slight sheen of sweat that made her flesh gleam like satin.

He imagined those darker bodies beside her, thick dark hair on hard chests and rigid erections sprouting from copious amounts of pubic hair.

Would one be in her mouth and one behind, he wondered? Would they change positions, each lying beside her, one pushing himself into her vagina while the other pushed in from behind?

He didn't know what their taste was likely to be. He could only visualise a naked Virginia, perhaps with her arms stretched, wrists bound high above her head. Dark heads before her breasts as each brother sucked on her nipples at the same time as their hands played with the roundness of her buttocks, the deep crease between, and the moist, aroused wetness of her sex.

On the other hand, he thought to himself, she could be the dominant factor in the triple liaison. That particular scene, of two male buttocks being paddled by her hand, a school teacher's cane or a huntmaster's whip, did not appeal to his own tastes, so was discarded from his mind.

With his cock now in his hand, his imaginings went back to the first scenario, one man in her mouth and one behind. As he thought on this, he felt his penis grow harder and a moistness spread over his palm.

He groaned as he worked the fingers of one hand up and down his member whilst the fingers of his other hand caressed his balls.

Just as if it were some woman riding him and he were meeting her thrusts, he jerked his hips up and down from the bed.

Faster and faster he worked his hand until he felt that familiar throbbing that told him his semen was rising, pulsing in the thick vein that ran up the back of his shaft.

At last, in one outpouring, it left his body and ran in a sticky mess over his hand and into a white handkerchief he had thought to have close by.

He lay still for a while afterwards, staring at the ceiling as if willing to see that rather than the vision in his head. But the thought was still there. Virginia was being screwed by two men at near enough the same time and he wasn't one of them.

Sighing almost painfully at the thought of what would not go from his mind, he turned over on his side and shut his eyes in an effort to blank out what she might be doing to them and what they might be doing to her. It had not worked. The vision of their copulation in a number of different positions stayed in his mind, turned into dreams, and the tension and hard-on it had left him with were still there in the morning.

Things had developed in Istanbul.

'I'm taking you on an evening tour of the city,' he had told Virginia. 'Be ready.'

She had laughed and told him her two Greek lovers had plans for her. She refused to tell him what they were.

'They have promised me their undivided attention,' she explained with a laugh. In her mind, she went through all the delicious things the Greek brothers had done with her.

212

It had been a novelty in itself to have had first one brother fuck her, then the other. The first had talked all the while; the other had watched. But the real novelty was in knowing that each was explaining to the other exactly what they were experiencing. It was weird, but strangely erotic, and she had not complained.

All night they had ridden as they chose. Best, she decided, had been her sucking Aristo while Ariel had entered her from behind. She had been surrounded by men, her body full of them, and her senses reeling from their touch, their scent, and their taste.

'I will go with them,' she said wilfully, then dropped her voice and came close to him. 'Remember, I have not yet fulfilled my mission.'

Raymonde made no comment. He just narrowed his eyes and looked at her as she walked away, black beads sparkling on her dress as she moved away from him with her hips swinging in an action that was designed to arouse.

Virginia did not know it, but she was definitely seeing Istanbul with him. Raymonde had made his mind up. If he had to orchestrate her being in his company, he would do so. That made it imperative he must first get rid of his rivals.

Having seen them playing cards back in the hotel in Paris, Raymonde found it comparatively easy to persuade both Zweizer, Davis and the twins that a game would be in order after lunch and before taking a tour of the city.

The two Greeks exchanged knowing looks, thinking this was a man with nothing like the natural penchant for card games they claimed to possess. Davis Sedglingham was always on the lookout for a way to make money, no matter what the means, and Zweizer, having paid off his wife's lover, was feeling light in his pocket. But the banker reasoned that he was entitled to indulge his own pleasures, just as he had in the best brothels of Europe, and just as his wife had with Hans who, unknown to her, was always well rewarded.

All of them looked on Raymonde, if not with contempt, then with the disdain those who had been on the voyage since its beginning had for a 'Johnny come lately'.

Unknown to the distinguished gentlemen who sat so smug yet so intent around the card table, Raymonde had learned about card management from a croupier back in one of the less honest casinos of Ontario and now came the chance to use this to good effect.

The opportunity came to cheat and Raymonde took it. He also made it look as though the Greeks were cheating Sedglingham and Zweizer.

Sedglingham, his pose incredibly arrogant as he smoked through a holder and held his head high as he peered at them with hooded eyes, was the first to complain.

'That can't be right. How can you have put the eight of clubs down if I have it here in my hand?'

Zweizer also noticed the same thing happening. Then it was the turn of brother against brother. Each accused the other of cheating. But no one accused Raymonde. He had worked the game so that cards seemed to appear after everyone else's play, never his own.

By the time Raymonde left the table, fists were swinging, noses were bloody and a bevy of carriage attendants were trying to break up the melee which included Aristo Kostopoles who now lay supine on the floor, his brother kneeling by his side, crying for him to wake up.

'I'm taking you up to Rumeli Hisar by moonlight,' Raymonde said firmly to a surprised Virginia as he grabbed her arm. 'It's a deserted fortress,' he explained.

'But Aristo and Ariel . . .'

'Are out cold,' he said abruptly.

By the time the day had passed and they had reached the crumbling fortress that overlooked the city, the mist down below had risen so high that only the roofs of the smaller buildings were showing.

Above them, a cloud passed over the face of the moon but did little to lessen its light.

Virginia had been a little piqued that she had missed her last chance at acquiring long-term security and sexual satisfaction. She had been winding up a gramophone and a deep frown had wrinkled her brow. As the sort of tune Fred Astaire usually danced to filled the cabin, Virginia narrowed her eyes.

'I said I was going sightseeing with the twins.'

'You can't,' Raymonde had responded. 'They're battered, bruised and the Turkish police are charging them with causing an affray on a Moslem holy day.'

'Are you kidding me?' she asked, hands landing on hips and elbows sharp.

'Honestly,' he said, and his smile was so warm, so full of enticement, that she had agreed to go with him. The Greeks' interest in her had been late in arriving. The wealth and sensual delights she had sought were now out of her grasp.

'Still,' she thought to herself as she responded to the scene and the feel of Raymonde's hand on her behind, 'at least I will still have the latter.'

Her hat fell to the ground as she tilted her head back so he could kiss her lips. She made no protest. On the contrary, she opened her mouth and felt a great thrill run down her spine as his tongue entwined with hers.

His hands pressed her buttocks more firmly so that her pubic region met the hardness of his cock.

Through the thin material of her shift, he played with her breasts and she squirmed as if she were trying to escape him when, of course, she was not.

He went on to run his hand up under her skirt until his fingers found the silkiness of her pubic hair and the moistness of her sex.

She moaned against his neck and wrapped her arms around him as his fingers dipped and slid in her juices. Her hips pulsed against him in an effort to draw him in, to have him inside her in any way at all.

A look of surprise came to her face as he suddenly held her at arms' length. She recognised the look on his face and the tone of his voice from that night on the train. And as she thought about what had happened she might even have blushed. On that night, she had bent over at his command to stare out of the window at the darkness outside.

'Take your clothes off,' he ordered.

She tensed and stared at him as if waiting for confirmation.

Moonlight caught the gleam in his eyes, the smouldering demand that was both menacing and exciting.

With trembling hands, her eyes still gazing into his, she did as ordered.

A cool breeze blew across that high place and caressed her body. It teased her nipples into hard prominence and delicately licked at her pubic hair.

'Turn round. Place your hands on the parapet – like you did on the train.'

Without saying a word, Virginia did just that. Her heart was beating faster. The blood was flowing hot and furious through her veins. Her senses were impatient for him, yet heightened by submitting to his command.

'Am I really doing this again?' she thought to herself. There was some surprise in the fact. Just the same as on the train, her breasts dangled beneath her, her legs were open and her bottom tilted out behind her.

Before lay a city rich in the flavours of east and west, both in food, culture and sensuality.

Behind her a man was easing himself into her. She groaned as his fingers dug into her flanks and she wriggled her bottom as his penis slid into her moist entrance.

As he pushed inside, her breasts swung and her breath caught in her throat until it almost sounded as though she were in pain.

216

But she was not in pain, she was in ecstasy.

At times she closed her eyes, but there was added delight in opening them, in seeing the city of some three million people below her and thinking that someone, some person looking out of a high window or from some flat roof, would see her and know what she was doing.

Her climax came with his, her buttocks pressing back into his groin to gain the last tremor from her orgasm.

In all the time he had been fucking her, she had not looked over her shoulder. She did not do that now, only mewed with contentment as he withdrew.

She murmured sweet, appreciative sounds and, just when she was about to turn round and perhaps arouse him again, he re-entered.

'Hi there, Ginny darling.'

She gasped. 'Emerson!'

As Emerson's penis went where Raymonde's had been before, the Canadian's face came into view. He was smiling.

'Well,' he said softly. 'You did say you wanted both security and sex. Emerson and I think we've got just the right arrangement for you – and for us!'

Breasts swinging, body swaying backwards and forwards, Virginia stared at him, mouth open.

'But . . .' she stammered before another thrust of Emerson's loins halted her words. 'What . . . about . . . Aust . . . ralia?'

'Bauxite!' cried Emerson. Such was his excitement that he came at the same time she cried out.

'Sold,' explained Raymonde as the Australian held position until the last drop of his essence had spurted into her. Raymonde kissed her cheek and she looked at him in wonder.

He continued, 'Emerson sold it for a fortune, so wherever you want to be is alright by him . . . by us.'

As a lesser orgasm ran through her body, Virginia began

to smile, her happiness adding to the pinkness of her flushed face.

'Do you mean that both of you . . .?'

Indeed they did. From then on, as the three of them travelled the world, the two men shared the sexiest woman they had ever encountered. As for Virginia, she revelled in the luxury of their bottomless wealth and the excitement of two handsome and ever-attentive lovers who knew how to satisfy her every desire.